"The boy who sailed to Spain"

By Paul O´Garra

First printed in English by Createspace,
an Amazon.com company.
Available from Amazon.com, Createspace.com and other retail outlets.
Also available On Kindle and other book stores also available from Ingram Sparks
and their worldwide network.

To the memory of my Mother

Teresita OGarra

who will never fade away from the memories of her children and of the
many who knew and loved her.

"The boy who sailed to Spain"

By Paul O´Garra

The chosen one.

The woman who lives in with us has gone to her family for the feast. Ramadan is now long past, and yet she's not returned. It sometimes happens; they are with us till we learn to love them, and then they go. But recently, it happens with all the servants. It's as if they had been told to stay away. We hope that soon, some of our own people will travel to us and stay to replace the ones who left. Now the Harira is brought in from the shop; it's not the same, but none of us say anything. Only Saul, the youngest, refuses to eat.

"Mama, why can we not eat Fatima's food, Mama, where is Fatima, when is she coming home?"

"Saul eat your food, leave your mother in peace. My father speaks with his gentle authority, he is strong, and everyone respects him. With his family, he is tender but also strict. My father says that a good father really must sometimes be hard in loving his people."

"I don't like the Harira, I won't eat it."

"You'll stay seated till it's eaten."

'Afra, he's just a boy; he misses her, we all miss her." My mother looks chidingly at him, 'Saul you will eat it, for me, please."

Later, I walk with my father into the street where the shops are. The wail of the muezzins tell people it's time for prayer and that Allah is watching over them. We visit the perfume shop where the aromas of azahar, jasmine, kalkan, patchouli, and millions of other flowers and herbs load the fresh night air with delightful scents that are carried away on the breeze.

Who knows what passing ships may pick up the wandering scent, where a traveller may notice it at tantalizing moments with a change in the direction of the evening breeze and wonder where it originated. One day, I will go away on a sailing craft to far off lands and will,myself, ponder at what strange people live in the towns on the darkening horizon.

'Papa, what's really happening?' I speak to him in English as I always do; he says it's the language of the world. He looks at me quizzically. 'It's not just Fatima and the house girls. I don't know, it's like a nervous tension in the air.'

'Masuhun, you are fifteen years old now; surely you understand. At school, reading the papers I give you, what you hear from your friends and the teachers. You're an intelligent boy.'

'You mean we don't fit, Papa. We are outsiders and it's coming to a head?'

He turned and clasped me, his eyes flashing. His easy-going mask slipped before my eyes, and I saw him as never before.

'Never say that, my beautiful son. We are the issue of a long, long line, and have lived here since time immemorial. From long before Islam was born, we have lived here, and we have been Christians since the time of the Romans.

'Masuhun!' He says my name loudly, 'Masuhun! I never told you, your name, the name your mother and I and your grandfather chose for you.' He still held me, pinning me ferociously by my arms as he looked into my eyes. I felt his strength. Many times, he had had to defend our shop against intruders I never understood, and here he was now, holding me and loving me, his eldest son. 'Your name means, "He who has been anointed."'

I felt the hairs bristle on the back of my head; why I don't know. It was as if all my daydreams about my destiny, the kind all boys have, were suddenly about to become true.

'Papa, does a name truly mean anything? After all, it is normally just a random choice or taken from other relatives of the same name.'

His mask had fallen back into place, and he again became the man of easy demeanour, gentle and patient; the man we all knew and held dear.

'What do we know, boy? What do we know? Only what is revealed to us. How many parents, upon discovering the meaning of the given name of their child, wonder how it is possible that the child bears most of the characteristics attributed to the name, to its meaning? I believe that in many cases the child already bore the name long before birth.'

'Salaam aleikum.' As we walked, we exchanged greetings with many people. Everyone was polite and kind. In the herb shop, the chameleons were sleeping on their tree. I could always spot them immediately. So many different herbs were all displayed in their hessian sacks ablaze with reds, oranges, greens, and hues of brown, and each with their own special aroma. The big, smiling giant of a man who ran the shop awarded me my three sticks of candy, one for each of us children. He didn't see we were growing up, he was just too busy smiling. One morning as I ran through the souk on an errand for my father, I came round a corner and found him sitting outside his shop, a big book in his arms, and with the first early rays of sun piercing through the roofs of the souk lighting him up, he chanted the mantras of the most holy Koran. Most of the shopkeepers were kind, some in a rough way, as they knew no better. It was a wonderful place to be brought up in.

We turned to go back home. It was time for Holy Mass and today it was our turn to be the house church. It was something we never mentioned outside of home for fear of persecution, although officially, where we lived, it was within the law to worship freely regardless of your creed. Not everyone agreed though, especially the authorities.

That night, late, they came again, many of them. When I heard voices raised in argument, I pulled on my robe and ran to the front of the house. As I peered from the balcony, I saw them around my father, striking him, and he was punching and knocking them down. There were so many, it was like a pack of hungry wolves worrying a buffalo. Screaming, I leapt from the house and threw myself at one and then another, flailing wildly with my fists, striking flesh and bone, but there was a blinding flash. Later my mother woke me with wails and kisses, followed by exclamations of relief when she saw I was alive. They told me he had fought like a tiger, but they'd left him for dead. The house was filled with men, cousins, uncles, and brothers. When I awoke, I screamed at them, 'Cowards, bastards, where were you when the killers came?'

They said he was dying. They had come, the Amazigh, our people, but they were too late. I ran crazily through the house, saying he was not dying; they wanted him dead, but he was not dying. I reached the bedroom where he lay, and they took me in to him. He spoke to me as I kissed him, asking him not to go.

'Masuhun, find the place on the stone where the blessed mother comes.'

I fought against the tears. I didn't want him to die; I wanted to walk with him, fish together, ride, sail; I just wanted to be with my father. I swiped angrily at my face—at the tears—but they were flowing fast and free now, blinding me.

'No papa, don't go; please, papa, papa, papa.'

'Masuhun, ask her to protect us again as before. She will listen to you, you are named for her son.'

That night, I swore on the sacred grave of my sainted murdered father that I, Masuhun al-Rasheed ibn Afra ibn Youssuf al Imazigen, would not rest until I had found the sacred rock, and knelt at the feet of the holy mother. I was just fifteen years of age, but fate had ordained that I should become a man.

The crossing.

You know how in spring, early in the morning, some days, you wake to find a blanket of white sea-mist hiding and muffling everything? The landscape becomes alien to you, and it's only as you start to pick out the occasional landmark that you remember where you are. I wasn't really in the mood for enjoying a mysterious start to the day; I wanted to get organised. I had packed a knapsack with provisions, some tins with easy opening tops, Berber bread, water, and a thermos with hot mint tea. I knew my mother, Saul, and my sister were safe, as several family members had moved in. My father had been taken to the hospital; I really didn't want to think about it, as it would water down my resolve. So I had come down to where my father kept the boats in a sort of sailing club on the beach that he had formed with some friends. A night watchman lived there, in a shed. I saw the boats, at least some of them, and then the shed loomed out of the mist. Further along the beach, a group of Africans were playing football. What they were doing playing at that hour was beyond me; maybe they were cold. There were many Africans all over, waiting for a ride or to devise a way to get to Europe and the West so they could realise their dream.

'Salaam Aleikum.'

'Aleikum Salaam Ali,' I replied. 'La bas alek?'

'Al hamdulilah. What are you doing up to so early, and where´s your father?"

'He will come in a while, I am going out now, help me Ali. I threw my bag onto the canvas tarpaulin which was the deck, as it were, of my craft. He followed me, shaking his head.

'I don't know, I don't know; there's mist and wind, and a strong levanter is coming in. Does your father know you are here?"

I needed to take control of the situation, so, much against my nature, I shouted at him.

'Who are you to question me? Help me and stop being stupid, or I will tell my father, and you will have to find yourself another job."

He sullenly gave in and wordlessly helped me as I hoisted the coloured sail and installed the double tiller and blades. I then locked on the pulley, which when attached with a rope to the sail, would allow me to play with the wind. The rope was long enough to allow the sail to go all the way to the en popa o transluchada positions. I had been taught to sail by a Spanish guy so it was bizarre, but I sailed only in Spanish; just like if you adopt a dog who lives with Russian people, well, the dog speaks only Russian. En popa was where you sailed before the wind, and the sail formed a sort of balloon. It was a marvellous way to relax, being pushed by a gentle wind; although you needed to be careful, as a strong sudden gust could well push the sail forward faster than the craft was moving, thereby forcing it under water or making it tip head over heels. So you held the sail, and you did not put the rope into the dientes de perro; you held it so as the gust came, you could relax the sail, let it go, so that the gust just swept past. The transluchada was the way of changing the direction the boat was travelling in by changing the side the sail was on, with the wind behind you, but when you made the change, the wind could well gust violently into the sail and overturn you. The safest way was the ceñida, o virada por avante which is changing into the wind. Here you can control the sail strictly as you change, so you are in no danger.

I tied my knapsack and warm jacket to the mast and put on the short neoprene wetsuit and life jacket. As I did, I remembered my father threatening to thrash me soundly if ever I put out without either. I put him out of my thoughts, as I could feel the tears coming, so I gruffly ordered Ali to lift. We carried the cat to the water's edge. The waves were pounding on the shore, but they were just levanter waves, all bark and little bite. We pushed her in a little. I got behind, gripping the rear bar and ready to push to launch the boat as Ali held her against the movement of the water. I had left the sail loose, but with the rope close to hand so I could instantly pull on it as I leapt aboard. As the last breaker spent its energy crashing onto the sand, I shouted, 'Ca va, ca va!'

We pushed her into the next wave and I leapt aboard, and dropping quick as a flash onto the right fin, sat facing the sail. With the wind coming from the front right of the boat, nor'westerly, I pulled the sail taut so that wind filled it, and suddenly the little craft was majestically riding the crests of the waves and out to sea in a ceñida sailing position, which is one of the fastest and most exciting.

I could hear Ali asking Allah to protect me. 'Allah soigne-le qui est seul un enfant et ne sache pas ce qu'il fait.' (Allah look after him as he is only a child and does not know what he is doing.)

So he knew, he knew this day was not like others, but he did not know why. Muslims are good people, like all others, although also like all others, amongst them are good and bad. Ali was one of the very good. He lived on the beach alone with his prayer mat on which he spoke to his God many times each day. Sometimes he bought meat from the boulangerie and made kefta on his makeshift fire. My father would buy chai nana, mint tea, and Berber bread. We would sit under a blanket spread to make a sunshade outside his shed and have the most delicious meal ever.

Then I saw that he was running along the beach waving and shaking his fist shouting, his chilaba blowing out behind him as he ran, but the wind took his words.

She was pulling to one side; I pushed the tiller over to right her, but nothing happened. Maybe the tiller was fouled. Then I saw him hanging onto the rear, his fists were big and closed on the bar and he just dragged out behind. It looked like one of those African fellows off the beach. The boat was pulled down at the back by the extra weight pulling on us, and the waves were starting to buffet us side on. She was just a tiny cat and the waves we had to climb to get out of the shore area were big. If I couldn't get her nose down and straighten her out so that she met the waves head on, we would be overturned. So I leapt forward, having fastened the sail, and jumped out onto the starboard hull as a counterbalance—like with a patin catalan, a sailing boat whose only steering mechanism is the sailor using his body weight. Well it worked;

we rode the breakers, albeit more sluggishly than usual. Out beyond the waves, where the swell diminished and the waves were wide, I relaxed the tension of the sail. The boat slowed down and the man clambered aboard. He seemed quite sheepish about things and didn't look me in the eye.

I shouted at him, 'Qu'est ce que tu veux? Es tu fou? Qu'est ce que tu fais?' (What are you doing? Are you crazy? What do you want?)

'I don't spik da lingo. I spik English.'

Thanks to my father, who always insisted we speak English at home and that we studied and read English classics and newspapers, English was as much my mother tongue as were Arabic and French.

'What do you want? Why have you come onto my boat?'

'My name is William. I have come all the way from Ivory Coast to get to da Europe, and here at da last step, I am held back by this beet of wata. And so I saw you and your bag, and I knew at once you are going to cross to da Europe.'

'Sorry, friend, better you return to the beach. I am going on a mission, a quest, from which perhaps I will not return.' Even as it came into my mind that I was being pompous, I knew I was speaking as much to myself as to him, and for the first time, I realized as I spoke that following my normal impetuosity, I had embarked on a voyage to cross one of the most treacherous stretches of ocean in the world. 'Jesus, be my light, help me,' I silently uttered, but it mustn't have been that silent, as William burst out.

'Then we are braadas, you and me. We are braadas. I also am a Christian. I will come with you. Together, we will be OK.'

'Are you a strong swimmer?' I asked him.

'Da best. I can swim like a shak, don you worry none abbaht William. I can swim foreber even in da heavy seas.'

I liked him; he was so natural. Pictures flashed before my eyes of William out at sea hanging onto a piece of wood, so I pulled the sail tight and laid her, side on, to the increasing wind. The cat suddenly went up onto one fin; a trick I had learnt and perfected with constant practice.

In fact, I could actually sail on one fin for as long as five minutes. William slid off the wet canvas and into the sea as the boat forged ahead.

'Why, my braada?' he wailed. 'Why you do dat?'

'Because you seem a nice man and I don't want you on my conscience. I will come to find you when I return,' I shouted, and whether he heard me or not I don't know. I did know, however, that he could easily regain the shore in just a matter of minutes. He was, after all, a swimmer as strong as a shak.

I sailed into the mist in the general direction of Spain, which is the southernmost country of the European continent. The wind had veered slightly and was coming from the general direction for which I was heading, so I needed to tack, which means changing direction every so often to maintain a reasonably straight course. People are surprised when they learn that sailing ships sail at the wind that powers them. Basically, it's a simple physical law, so that as the wind hits the sail, if this is set slightly to one side, the energy you anticipate would drive you backwards actually powers you forward, albeit on a sideward tack, hence the term tacking.

Slowly, the mist began to lift, and I could see Spain far off, appearing and disappearing. The boat was making little headway, as due to the heavy head winds, it would be tacking all the way. I came out from behind the shelter of land and was exposed full on to the Atlantic on my left. The swell was massive here, so that the land ahead in the distance appeared and disappeared, though now not because of the mist, which had gone, but because of the big troughs I sank down into as my small boat rode the waves. The wind was also much stronger, so I needed to concentrate all the time, which was quite exhausting. The hours passed. The sun was beating down, and I was grateful it was not yet summer. I began to have some doubts; the seas were so heavy and I was so tiny. Don't be a wimp, I told myself. Jesus is with you, God is with you. Rather than going forward, I realised the cat was moving west and rather than getting closer, the land seemed to be moving away.

The sun started to go down. The seas seemed to calm down a little, reacting to the thermic effect, the cooling down of the sea and the land ahead. Suddenly, I knew it would be dark soon and I would be lost in the night without even a light. I put on my warm jacket, which was now wet through, and tied myself to the mast. I was so afraid I felt like crying, but remembered I had promised the tears I had shed for my father would be the last until I came to the place of the Lady where my father had sent me. Any big ship passing would run me down or I would be caught up in its propellers. I asked the Lady, the mother of Jesus, to intercede for me to keep me safe. I was freezing, my teeth were chattering, and I was so very tired.

I awoke suddenly with a jump. It was pouring, with the rain sheeting in clouds that were pushed across the surface of the sea by the wind. I could see all of this thanks to a big beam of light cutting through the darkness directly at me and blinding me. The foghorn that had startled me out of my sleep sounded again, and again startled me. Shielding my eyes against the beam, I saw a rope that was attached to something snake across the water and land on the other side of the cat. I knew I was being pulled towards the vessel, some sort of a grapple hook or something must have been on the end of the rope. A man was gripping a ladder on the side of the big boat as he gestured to me. At the same instance, a voice blared out of a megaphone.

'Catamaran, as you approach us, grab the ladder. The seaman will help you.' Then it repeated the same thing again and again.

Easier said than done. As the cat came closer, the other vessel was shifting with the heavy swell. Somehow, I grabbed the ladder, but the cat squashed my leg against it violently. I screamed, but the man on the ladder had me and pulled me up by the armpit, somehow getting his bearlike arm around me. Other men took me from him and pulled me up to safety.

Once inside, someone took my wet clothes. I still had my neoprene on, so I dried with a big stiff towel and curled up in the blankets they gave me. Then I took off my wetsuit under the blanket, which made them laugh, and they made comments in a
language that seemed like Spanish or Portuguese.

'Are you all right, boy? Que tiene escondio picha? What have you got hidden there?' They all roared with laughter.

'Yes, thank you,' I politely replied, which set them off again speaking their language with bits of English thrown in. I knew they were joking with me, but they were men; men who worked and sweated and sailed, who loved their women and children.

'How'd you get here, boy? It's a long way from the beach. What happen, el perkins te fallo? Your diesel engine have problems?' Again, they all laughed raucously. Another asked my name and where I was from. I suppose it was a novelty for them to have a newcomer on board, especially one fished out of the ocean. A big man came in, and as they stopped asking me things, I decided he must be the captain. He came over to me, took my head in his big hand, and looked into my face.

In a deep sonorous voice, he said, 'My name is Frank. I am skipper here. What is your name?'

'Masuhun, sir. Thank you for saving me. I don't want to appear ungrateful, but is my boat safe?'
'You are safe and that is all that is important. But yes, your boat, we slung several lines over and have secured her. Jimmy, give the boy, Masuhun, hot tea and something to eat.'

'Aye, Skipper.'

'When you feel better, come up to see me on the bridge, Masuhun. I want to talk with you.'

'Yes, skipper,' I said.

Well, they gave me tea, lots of it, and food. The tea was incredible though very different from the mint tea I was used to. The men told me it was tea that had won many wars, and I believed them, although I also knew it had caused at least one. The one called Jimmy looked at my leg and said it was OK. He put cream and a bandage on it. Then he cleaned the wound above my eye and put cream and a dressing on it. That wound had happened at the house, but I never knew it.

I clung onto the brass bannister as I made my way to the bridge. The ship was lurching and throwing everything from side to side. Thank God they found me, or I'd be out there. I felt cold and shivered at the very thought.

The skipper was standing at a window gazing out to sea. The visibility was good, as the windows had wipers that fought valiantly against the rain and heavy spray. We could see the progress the ship made against the heavy seas as she staggeringly lifted her head, only to fall again into the next trough.

'Tell me, Masuhun, what were you doing sailing a catamaran on high seas?'

'I was on the beach, and I sailed out and must have fallen asleep.'

'Tomorrow, I will hand you and your boat over to the Spanish authorities, or to the Gibraltar police, so if you want to help me decide what is to be done, you must tell me the truth. ¿Dormido, dice el niño que se quedó, tú la oído? Mañana, we put in y avisamos al Spanish authorities, de chulería nada.' (Asleep, the boy says he fell asleep, you heard him. Tomorrow, we put in and advise the Spanish authorities, no clever stuff.)

'Hombre Frank, es un chaval.' (Frank, man, he's just a kid.) This was the helmsman who spoke. I more or less caught the gist of what was being said, although it seemed like a mix of English and Spanish.

'Por mu chaval que sea, coño casi naufraga, y ahora no quiere hacer a clean breast of it.' (Sure he might be a young lad, but he nearly was shipwrecked, and now he won't make a clean breast of it.)

I spoke up in a small voice, as he seemed to be getting quite angry. 'My father sent me.'

'No. No father would send you to do such a reckless thing. Don't say silly things, boy.'

'He didn't know I would come in this way. He was dying and he told me to go to Europe to find the mother.'

'¿Sera verdad?' (Can this be true?)

'Escúchalo, Frank joder. Allí en frente pasan muchas cosas.' (Listen to him, Frank. Hell. Over there on the other shore, many things happen.)

'How long ago was this?'

'Yesterday. He died yesterday. They killed him.'

'Shit.' The skipper looked at the seaman who was steering, and they exchanged glances.

'You don't believe me.'

The skipper sat down and took a pipe from his pocket. 'Sit down, boy.' He looked at me. 'Please.'

Then he took a packet from his other pocket and slowly and deliberately started to fill his pipe. Only when he had finished and lit it did he look at me again. 'Who did this?'

'We don't know. Many men; they came by night. I tried to stop them. Afterwards, the Amazigh came, but it was too late; he was already badly wounded. He told me to find the mother. My grandfather had once told me of the mother, and that she was in Europe.'

'Who're the Amazigh?'

'My people.'

'And where will you go to find this mother; whose mother is she, anyway?'

'She is the mother of the anointed one. I am named for him.'

The steersman looked at the captain. 'Skipper, I think he means Mary. The anointed one is the Messias, her son. Messias means the anointed one. Esta hablando de María y Jesús.' (He's talking about Mary and Jesus.)

'My grandfather says she protected us before, many hundreds of years ago, when Christians were being slaughtered. We have been Christians since more than one thousand years, since the Romans, since the times of St Augustine of Hippo.'

'Masuhun, go now and sleep, ask Jimmy to give you a berth. Tomorrow, we will see what is to be done.'

As I left the bridge, I could hear them talking.

'¿Oye Freddie, y el Augustine de hippo quien fue?' (Hey Freddie, and who was that Augustine of Hippo?)

So I went and slept till the change in the movement of the boat woke me. I said a prayer of thanks, as I knew I was in Europe and closer to the Mother.

El Coto Doñana.

I stepped off the ship's ladder onto the cat. She was quite shipshape, as Jimmy and I had checked everything before we refloated her. I glanced up at the bridge. Frank, the skipper, put his hand to his cap in a salute, and I saluted back. He looked grim, unsmiling. I wondered if it was me or perhaps he was just one of those people who wake up in a bad mood. I didn't want to have this unsmiling memory of someone who had done so much for me and had been so good, so I upturned my arms enquiringly. Then he smiled. It made me feel happy and warm inside, and I smiled back; the biggest, widest smile I could muster as I mouthed the words 'Thaaaaank you, thank you, skipper.'

He responded by waving a finger at me in what was meant to be a make sure you behave gesture, then the loudspeaker crackled. 'Find the lady, boy, and be careful. Don't do anything too rash.'

I cast off the line that was still holding the cat to the side of the vessel, let the sail out to catch the wind, and she spun off gleefully. I put her onto one fin a couple of times and waved at the seamen. Overnight, the weather had changed, and it was a beautiful sunny day. The storm had blown itself out and a fresh delightful Poniente was blowing from Africa. The crew waved as I sailed towards the beach. Looking back, I had my first view of the vessel. I had come onto her at night and so had not really seen her. She was snub-nosed and black, with winches and thick hawsers lying all over her. A real working girl, Frank had told me, and she was beautiful lying there in the sunlight. Then I saw her name written in gold and black letters on her side, MV Maria, and below that, as port of origin, Gibraltar. So she had heard me. I was so afraid, but she was there with me all along. When they found me, they were on a return run from England, Portsmouth, a big English port. They had towed a ship there and were coming home. That they found me at all was, as Jimmy termed it,

'Un milagro. A miracle. Masuhun, t'aparecio la virgin (The virgin appeared to you.) I think it was a Spanish saying, but he was so right, the mother had intervened for me.

The beach was quite close now and deserted, except for the occasional fisherman.

I hit the sand side on so the wind would not tip me over in the few seconds before I released the sail once on land. I started to pull her up the sand, but she was a bit heavy for one. A man came over from where he was fishing and said, 'Pesa mucho.' (Very heavy.)

I said yes, 'Sí.' But my Spanish vocabulary and use of the language were very rusty, so I told him, 'English.'

He said, 'Ohh, engleesh. No engleesh.' He smiled and gestured, then walked up the beach towards where the dune grass was growing and came back pulling on a rope over his shoulder. All the while, he spoke to me and explained in signs. We were going to pull her up using his ancient wooden winch. It worked with a bar that he inserted across the top and we pushed and pulled so that the cat came up the sands. Once she was right up and safe from tides and future storms, we sat on one of her fins and he smoked a smelly cigarette he called 'mis ducados' as we drank water from my knapsack. Jimmy had replenished my stores with fresh sandwiches and hot tea in the thermos flask.

Later, I found the small house where Frank had sent me.

'I don't really know them,' he said. 'But they seem good people. I'm sure if you mention my name, they will let you stay at least for a night.'

So I knocked on the door. It was a small whitewashed sort of terraced cottage with a smart new door and windows. On either side were shabbier houses, but their gardens were resplendent with colour from the many lovely plants growing in beds, pots on windowsills, and hanging from the walls. The house I was to be visiting was in the deep shade, whereas the neighbours were flooded with warm sunlight, making it seem ominous and threatening somehow. I looked behind myself to see that the culprit was just a big tree blocking the light. I pressed the doorbell and heard a chime within. The door was opened by a lady of some forty years. I say forty because she was fat and I could not really judge her age. I just knew for a fact that she wasn't twenty-one or twenty-five or anything. She could have been forty or fifty or even sixty. So I decided to think of her as being forty, and see how she evolved as I got to know her.

'¿Que quieres?'

'English,' I replied.

'Paco, un ingle, un guiri.' (Paco, an English guy.) A tall skinny man with a large Adam's apple suddenly appeared beside her, well above her and to one side. He sort of craned his neck over her shoulder and looked at me quizzically, peering over the top of a pair of glasses.

'Spik eengleesh pleez?'

'Yes, sir. Frank sent me. Frank said you would give me a bed for one night and look after my catamaran.'

'¿Que dice, que dice?' the fat lady chimed in. 'Que a mi me parece un guiri muy raro. Parece gitano o moro. De guiri poco. ¿Que e lo que te a dicho Paco?' (What's he saying, what's he saying? He seems a very strange looking English to me. He looks Gypsy or Moroccan. Nothing English about him. What did he say to you Paco?)

'Dice que su padre es Aleman, y que están en San Lucar, y que se quiere quedar una noche a dormir.' (He says his father is German, and he is in San Lucar, and he wants to stay one night to sleep.)

'¿Y porque no se va con su padre?' (And why doesn't he go with his father?)

'Porque el niño se vino en un barquito y no puede volver, y que mañana viene su papi a por el.' (Because the boy came in a small boat and cannot return, and tomorrow his father will come to fetch him.)

'¿Y porque aquí?' (And why here?)

'Porque 1 án mandao mujer. Tantas preguntas, parece una civila.' (Because they have sent him, woman. So many questions, you are like a female Civil Guard.)

'¿Y quien la mandao?' (And who sent him?)

'El cura, la mandao, el cura.' (The Priest, the priest sent him.)
'Con el cura voi habla yo.' (I am going to have words with the priest.)

The fat woman went back into the house, pushing the tall man, who dodged so that she stumbled and nearly fell. I was quite worried, as it seemed as if they were arguing or something about me.

'Is it all right?' I asked timidly.

'Yes, all right, don't worry.' Then he gestured at me with a crooked finger, beckoning me closer. I put my ear forward. 'Don't say the name Frank here. She don't like him.'

'What do you mean? Frank is a nice good man,' I whispered back.

'She says he takes me to meet bad women; he is a bad influence.'

'Does he?' I was quite shocked.

'I take him,' he whispered. 'He don't wan come, but he come. Also we play cards and drink. Listen, boy, what your name?'

So I told him my name, and he said we had to go to see the priest to tell him the same story as he had told his wife or there would be trouble.

'Beeg trouble, Masuhun. La Debo, she is like weetch.'

So I told him a little of my story; just that I was seeking a talisman and that it involved historical churches in the region.

'A talisman, yes.' Then as he winked knowingly at me, I wondered what he was thinking. 'And they send a boy. It looks better, no one suspects. So I will phone my cousin Pepe and a couple of friends. They have contacts, they will help. Wait here, Masuhun.'

I hated the idea of cronies and phoning friends and cousins. My father would always discuss with us if he was going to ask or do a favour, as he did not want to be unfair to others. And it was a rare occasion anyway. He always warned against joining clubs or societies with a view to currying favour or meeting new powerful friends. Friends are for friendship, not for preferment, he would always say, and the rest is in the hands of God. I would have taken Paco on good faith and tried to find the road with his help, but not in this way. So I went back to the beach where I had met the old man. He was by the shore still fishing. He looked at me questioningly with open hands.

'¿Que paso?' I took him by the arm and drew a church in the sand and a woman with a baby. Why, I don't know. He just gave me a sense of tranquillity. He was just an old man with whom I could scarcely communicate, and whom I had just met. But there was something about him that inspired my trust.

'Maria?'

'Maria,' I said. In our tradition, we never named the mother, but here she was named Mary, as the steersman had said, or Maria. Just like the MV Maria.

'Sí, Maria,' I said. He took the stick from my hand and wrote 0700 in the sand. I said tomorrow, and he nodded. We laughed and he repeated.

'Tamorau, tamorau.' His name was Amador and his boat was also named Amador. We went back to casting his lines for a while. He taught me how to bait the hook and cast the line so that you could see it arcing through the evening sky, landing far beyond where one would expect it to, with just the slightest of splashes.

I left Amador as it was getting dark. As I neared the house again, I saw what looked like police, a jeep outside the house, so I instinctively hid. I knew nothing of the police in this country, but if the ones at home were anything to go by, it would be better to avoid them. A uniformed man was standing by the open vehicle, smoking. Youngish, with short hair and a long drooping moustache, he looked around as if waiting for someone. I heard a rustle in the bushes, and Paco's long mournful features appeared. He was holding a finger to his lips, cautioning silence.

'La Debo, she call her nephew, Julian. He is with the Guardia Civil. She is suspicious, think you are terrorist or thief. You sleep in shed tonight so they think you go.'

So he led me along the road to a makeshift wooden shed. I carried my bag and things, even the sandwiches Jimmy had made for me. Inside the room was a bed with a blanket, so I would be OK for the night, I mused.

And then Paco closed the door behind him. I could hear that his breathing was louder and faster. Through the window, the moonlight flooding in illuminated his face, which had taken on an evil, lascivious leer. He extended an arm to touch me. 'You are so beautiful.'

I had never contemplated whether I was attractive to look at or not; after all, I was a boy and not a girl. In our world, boys became men, and their worth was based on how they lived and behaved. What was happening was not good, so I dodged and arm-blocked his arm with mine, then I kicked right towards where I knew it would hurt. He just collapsed in a heap, squealing.

'Why, why?' he screeched.

I grabbed my things and made for the door, grasping the blanket I had pulled off the bed. 'Because I am fifteen and must decide my own paradigms in life, as also my own nature. And I don't really understand, but think you wanted to abuse your power over a helpless rabbit, who, sadly for you, has teeth.'

I ran from the shed down towards where I knew the beach would be after having locked the man into his own shed. It was about a kilometre or so to where I could see the Amador silhouetted in the moonlight. The boat was covered with makeshift canvas awnings that I pulled back so I could climb in. It smelled of old fish, hemp rope, old canvas, and boat oil. It was an incredibly clean odour, honest and normal. I pulled the canvas sheets back over the boat, and covered myself with the blanket against the night cold blowing off the sea. I unwrapped the sandwiches and ate them hungrily, then fell asleep, a slumber full of knights in white tunics and something bad and slithery insinuating itself into the dream only to have its head lopped off. There was also a beautiful woman with a child.

I woke with a start, and looked around. It was black, pitch black. For a few seconds, I couldn't remember anything till the smell of old fish and ropes brought it all rushing back. The sea made a murmuring sound that, as I listened, became waves gently breaking on the shore. Then I could feel someone moving the canvas coverings.

'Buenos días, muchacho.' Amador smiled in at me. He didn't seem very surprised to see me sleeping in his boat, more like he had just pulled back the coverings to wake me.

'Nos vamos,' he gestured, and helped me collect my bag and the blanket. We hurried over to a very old, squarish, small blue van-like car with small letters on the doors telling people what I imagined was her name. He confirmed it by pointing at himself and stating 'Amador,' then pointing at the car as he slapped it affectionately.

'El Tremendo. Se llama El Tremendo.' (The tremendous one.)

So we started. To where, I knew not, in the company of an old man with whom I could scarcely communicate, and in a foreign country where the little I remember of its language was just very slowly beginning to come back to me. I was happy, though. I was on my way, had found a friend, and had Maria and her son to protect me.

Sanctuary.

Amador drove safely, but slowly. Every half an hour or less, we made a stop for him to smoke a ducados. He had a problem with bridges, and went round them, never across. When I challenged him one of the times he turned off as we approached an overhead, saying, '¿Amador, que pasa bridge?' he just laughed and waved a hand in the air.

I had no idea where we were going till I started to see the place name Algeciras again and again. It was an untidy, ugly, industrial type of scenario with warehouses, lots of lorries, and spaghetti junctions. It was a relief to finally turn off the main highway onto a side road. After some 100 metres, a nondescript sign appeared indicating Ronda, Castellar, and Jimena. As we went gradually up into the hills, the scenery changed dramatically into wide rolling expanses, lush fields, and hillsides, replete with cattle. Then there were even bigger fields planted with grain, wheat, and hay; the wheat stalks, still green but heavy with mazorkas, swayed rhythmically in the wind. The contrast to the road we were on earlier was remarkable. Thank God our destination wasn't Algeciras. Grandiose, elaborate gateways led to unseen stately haciendas and estancias that, in my imagination, would be nestled in protected valleys, hidden from the main road. You could see stables, and now and again training fields. We saw proud horses and normal working farm horses, and once even a mini bullring. This could well be matador terrain, wild bull country.

My father had often spoken to me of one mad summer when he went with his father to a town called Pamplona in the Basque north of Spain. He gave his father the slip in the evening and ran with the bulls. It was an honour, a tradition of man against the wild animal. My father said that today, the same illness destroying the west could be seen at Pamplona, where alcohol, drugs, lust for money, and lewd sexuality in all its forms had reduced the proud Basque tradition to a drunken orgy. A shell of what he once experienced.

We passed through rolling measureless hills, pastures for the skulking dangerous, yet beautiful, beasts. There would be vast haciendas where the legendary toro bravo was initially nurtured before being led out to pasture on his enormous domain, there to gain strength as he grew to young adulthood and his terrible future.

We reached a crossroads and carried on to Castellar and Jimena, leaving San Martin del Tesorillo, proudly identified by its roadside sign, off to the right. Amador needed to stop, so we went into a very rustic looking roadside tavern. I sat outside, where a man came and sat with me. He was old, and for some reason, he had an air about him that said donkey keeper. So I asked him

'Señor, donkeys, burros?'

He replied with a smile. 'I speak English. And yes, I am friendly with donkeys and asses, burros y asnos.' I didn't dare say anything, but he sounded just the like Frank the tugboat skipper when he spoke.

'Do you know this area well, sir?'

He nodded assent and smiled, so I continued. 'I just need to know if there's a stone here with a sacred mother holding a child.'

He pondered for a while.

'Amador told me you would ask.'

'Oh, sorry, I didn't know you were friends.'

'No, you were too intrigued by my donkey smell.'

'No, sir.' I started forward. 'I really meant no disrespect.'

'I know that,' he chuckled. 'Anyway, you were very right. How the devil you knew is beyond me. I do live with donkeys, you see, you must be a very intuitive person.

'Let me tell you what I know of the sacred mother you seek. In the year 711, a Berber general, Tariq Ibn Zayd, invaded the peninsula and defeated the Visigoth king Roderic. Arab rule was subsequently established and lasted for hundreds of years. In 1309, King Ferdinand the fourth, accompanied by Don Alfonso, Don Alvaro Perez de Guzman, and other nobles, expelled the Arabs from Gibraltar, a rock at the southernmost point of the peninsula and crucial to Arab military domination. Ferdinand gave thanks to the Lord for his victory and dedicated Europe, Christian Europe, to the mother of Jesus under the title of our Lady of Europa. An ancient mosque at the very tip of Gibraltar was converted into a shrine to the mother of God, and a statue sculpted in limestone was venerated there. Twenty-four years later, the Arabs, conscious of the essential strategic importance of this rock, recaptured it. The inhabitants of the fortress, devoted to and fervent in their belief in the virgin, carried this effigy in holy procession to Castilian dominated land and safety, in spite of tremendous odds and in courageous defiance of the invading forces.'

'Faith really does move mountains,' I murmured, caught up in the tale.

'Just think of it,' he said. 'Those little Christians carrying the object of their faith, an effigy made of limestone, probably by sculptors of the most humble origins. All around them seeing killing, hearing horrendous screaming, fighting, and armed mounted Arab warriors brandishing scimitars. With dignity and showing no fear, singing in praise and glorification of the mother, they marched in procession all through this. And not a hair on the head of any participant in that procession was harmed.'

Amador arrived and we sat for a while. I sat in silence, just thinking, whilst they drank a beer and chatted. When Amador and I headed back to the car, the man followed us to see us off, then took me by the arm.

'Good luck, boy. Your friend will take you now to see her. The virgin disappeared for some 400 years after this procession, until she was found in a niche behind a curtain in the old convent. Today this nunnery is a church, a sanctuary to a virgin that the locals have named La Señora de los Angeles. Yes, Masuhun, she is the virgin that originally came in the procession from the shrine on the rock.'

It was evening time, and the sky was darkening quickly as we entered the sanctuary gates. There was singing and the little chapel was filled with the devout, women with their heads covered by veils, old men, and children. I walked right up to the altar and saw the statue of a woman holding a baby. The scent of recently collected flowers and incense filled the shrine as I slowly knelt down and asked her to help my father, but deep inside, I knew my quest was not over and that I needed to go to the shrine, the rock or stone, and then she would answer me. The village women just left me there, as they knew I was thinking of her. Then I stood up and walked out.

I awoke in front of the sanctuary, holding myself, rolled in a ball as if such actions would fend off the cool of the night. Something had disturbed me. It was still dark, and apart from the night noises, there was a rustling accompanied by the sound of heavy steps and dragging. I curled up tightly and tried to blend more effectively in the shadow of the fence against which I was sheltering. I must have been in that position for ages when at last I noticed, as in a dream, the faintest suggestion of dawn in the pitch black surrounding me. Then I heard a cock crow, again, and again, and the words, uninvited and unthought of, flitted across my mental vision, 'I would never betray you.' In the slowly rising dawn, I was able to discern a figure hooded in the Arab way and wrapped in what appeared to be heavy robes—a chilaba, maybe, or some sort of cassock. It stopped, facing me in the darkness, then sat slowly down as if with great difficulty or pain on the bench.

'Puedes salir ya.' (You can come out now.) It was the voice of a woman, probably very old. It brought to mind the old Berber women of the desert who lived in tents and had great wisdom. I had often gone there with my father to visit them. In my reduced condition, my earlier apprehension had gone, so resigned, I emerged slowly, shivering and in a trancelike state induced by the cold and lack of sleep.

'Here sit with me.' She leaned forward to loosen a blanket that was slung over her shoulder and handed it to me. I wrapped its thick folds around my body, and slowly, the shivering spasms decreased. She raised her hand to put me at ease, and in the oblique twilight, I thought I could make out a smile. Her face seemed to be wrinkled in every way, her eyes, forehead, cheeks were all creased to the extreme, her features coloured a light but intense Bedouin brown. When she smiled, all her stern demeanour seemed to lift as if it had been a veil. The first furtive rays of sunlight showed me her eyes, which were a vivid green and shone so that I just stared, drawn in by her ancient enigmatic beauty.

'Are you an angel? How did you know I was there?'

'No, bless you. Just a very old woman. I knew because your fear was speaking to me. Human beings are equipped with great telepathic powers; sadly, they will disappear over the millennia if not used vigorously. You are different, as are so many of the children of the so-called third world. You have been kept apart from all the technological instrumentation of today so that your body is aware of its wakening powers, although only subconsciously. Of course, the powers that be are rapidly ensuring that the whole of humanity, even those made less fortunate by the geography of their nations, falls prey to their telephones, computers, and as much of their technological poison as they can muster. Poison that, administered in limited doses with proper controls, would be a blessing.

'How strong is your faith, boy?'

I was taken aback. Perhaps she had already mentally touched my mind with thoughts of betrayal. 'My faith, Mother? I believe in all that my parents have taught me, what I learnt from the church, catechism. I believe that my parents have always done their best to lead us along the right path.'

'No!' her eyes blazed, and her voice became hard. 'Your faith, boy! Tell me about your faith! Your faith!'

I didn't really understand what she wanted, so I told her what had happened. I told her of the sea trip and the Maria.

'Do you know what happened here? How many Arabs fought and died over this holy land, inspired by their prophet and the idea that they were sent by God? And how many Christians, Visigoths, Spaniards, and Knights Templar shed their blood, fought to the last man, possessed with faith? They lived their lives for their beliefs, the sincere ones; and so many were sincere, fervently true to their unyielding faith, their God, and what they believed he wanted of them. It may well have been a natural event, a territorial war or series of wars, a shifting of cultures, and the complicated algorithms of the balance of power. But time has shown me that the gods we worship are all the same God and that we should all worship together, each in his own way.' She carried on speaking, but with such clarity and passion that I was mesmerised.

'The first requirement in this enlightened era of a passionate and real faith is to create a truth, to build a truth on that faith by learning to wisely discern between good and evil. To build a truth that will be the paradigm of good and to identify the devil, evil, in its multiple disguises. Only then, by teaching others to pass on this word, by using every device to again amass the armies of the Lord, can we bring the light of God back to the world.'

'Why are you telling me, all this? I don't really follow, but it seems that you think people with a strong faith should question everything, everything they see and hear, and becoming aware, must try to make others aware.'

'Masuhun? Masuhun, is that not your name?'

I was amazed and frightened. How could this old lady know me? It was uncanny, and the hairs on my arms stood on end. What was happening?

'How do you know me, my name?' I stuttered and stood, getting ready to bolt. She quietened me, and I fell back onto the bench as she spoke words such as my father had just a few days ago.

'Do you know the meaning of your name, Masuhun?'

I replied what my father had told me. 'I am named for the anointed one, the baby in the arms of the mother, the child who was Jesus of Nazareth, the Messias.'

'I am telling you all this because you are chosen to follow the road of reason, to find your way and teach others to build a new truth. You are one of many upon whom the notion and subsequent conviction has already fallen or will fall, in all corners of the world. It is your collective faith that will be the new chance for mankind to survive and live up to the expectations of the Creator.'

I shivered in my blanket and looked at her; it was all a bit above my head, like a dream.

'Are you like me, then? What are you?'

'I am a Jewess who left everything to be with the mother. I was born amongst English speaking peoples many years ago. Understand that you will have a journey and you will see evil. You are armed to recognise it and disarm it, but the devil is insidious and clever. You will suffer and know great fear, and many will seek to harm you and speak evil of you because of your faith. You will think yourself right when you are wrong and wrong when you are right. Think of the son of the mother and follow his path.'

We sat there in silence for a time as I absorbed what she had been saying. I must have dozed off. I shook the sleep from my head and looked for her, but she was gone and so was the blanket.

Caños de Mecca.

I wandered aimlessly around the empty and echoing streets of the tiny town. The last human contact I'd had was with the old woman, and I wondered if she had just been part of a dream. The old man, Amador, had completely disappeared—so completely that it seemed as if, having brought me here, he had deemed his mission complete. Well, in fact it was over, it had been wonderful of him to bring me so far anyway. But I was so alone that I ached physically inside; I suppose I missed his silent smiling companionship. I saw a strange unkempt man on a bench and thought of sitting down with him, sharing the bottle he was swigging from, till I realised I could not speak proper Spanish, I was still too rusty. A stray dog sniffed at my foot but snarled viciously when I tried to caress him. I began to despair inside, the awful despair of the lost. Then I remembered what had happened when I had thought I was lost at sea. How could I forget to believe in such a short time? I was not alone; my loneliness was but an illusion. And as if to illustrate my thoughts, the ground around me began to vibrate as the booming of heavy metal music, or something, approached. The bench dweller stood up abruptly, cradling his bottle defensively as he hissed out utterances in the general direction of the growing cacophony. A big van came slowly round the corner blasting the metal music out of big speakers fixed on its roof. A jumble of surfboards, bicycles, and general paraphernalia was piled on the roof and hanging from fixtures on the sides of the vehicle. I peered inquisitively as it very gradually eased to a stop right by me. A door slid open and two boys and a girl swung out. The interior seemed to be as cluttered with young people as the roof was with surfboards. The smaller one of the boys, a thin very dark-skinned individual, looked at me questioningly.

'¿Tío tiene algo?' (Man, have you got anything?)
I looked at him blankly, and the girl said, 'Hierba, hierba?' (Grass, grass?) She spoke loudly, like she thought I was deaf.

So I answered, 'English, please.'

The second boy, larger, plump, and with one of those ever friendly faces, retorted. 'Ingleesh, please. ¿El hijo puta? ¡Solo Ingleesh, el cabron!' With that, he started giggling. I realised they were drugged, smoking hashish. In my country, only old men did this. The girl joined in, and some of the people inside the van poked their heads out. The big boy kept making comments, and soon everyone was giggling. Even the tramp off the bench was offering his bottle and making strange choking noises.

'Come with us, man,' the first boy said as he indicated with his head that two uniformed men were walking towards us.

'Police?' I enquired.

He just shrugged, so we all crammed into the van and sped off out of town.

Through the night, the van motored smoothly on bright new motorways with silky gentle surfaces whilst its occupants, in the main, had been swept surreptitiously into the arms of Morpheus, or marijuana. They slept, some with the intensity and disregard that only the young and secure possess. Others slept more fitfully, and a young good-looking guy in a corner fondled a girl whilst another boy seemed to be fondling him. Beside me, the lad I had met who had invited me along was slumped, and others were strewn around in a haphazard fashion, legs and arms randomly interlaced or covering a part of their neighbour's anatomy that did not suffer resultant discomfort. I must have dozed off, as my eyes opened to folks around me starting to wake, yawn, and chatter.

'My name is Ruben.' One boy looked at me and held out his hand. 'Hello, Masuhun. Hey, this is David, and this boy here is not really a boy, she's a girl, Maria.'

She threw a shoe in reply, which Ruben deftly dodged before going on. 'This here is Claudio, you met him outside before; this is Maria two, or you can call her Maria la guapa, the pretty one, to distinguish her from Maria one; and then there's Juan; Lanzarote; and Eduardo in the corner, part of the Juanito, Eduardo, and Toñi trio.'

Some nodded as they heard their names spoken, although it seemed that most had at least a rudimentary command of English, though they pretended not to.

'¿Que quiere decir con eso de trio?' (What's that about a trio meant to mean?) Eduardo asked. He was a big guy, sculpted from time in the gym. But Ruben just ignored him.

Then the girl Toñi joined in. 'Sí! ¿A que viene el meterte con Eduardo? ¿Además quien es tu nuevo amiguito? ¿Un mendigo, un sin techo buscavidas? ¿Que es, que, te cuesta encontrar amigos? ¿Además quien le dijo que podía subir al furgón?' (Yeah, what's with you digging at Eduardo? So who's your new friend? A waif, wandering bum? You hard up for friends? Who said he could come on the bus?)

She got quite carried away. I was getting worried and could see myself getting unceremoniously kicked off. Ruben looked at me with a totally deadpan face, then he gave me a hidden wink. Claudio piped in, and then the others. It seemed like there was a self-appointed elite faction made up of the trio, with Claudio and Maria two as the hangers-on. Speaking to me in English, Claudio asked me questions, but would cut me off as I replied to make a comment in Spanish to his clique. They would laugh, and it certainly wasn't with me. Ruben threw in his bit now and then to set them all off squabbling again. Lanzarote, a good-looking, fair-haired giant from Bilbao just sat there grinning. Ruben told me of Lanzarote's claim to fame, he had rescued a girl from a beating in Tangiers only to discover she was not a girl, she was a guy. Lanzarote just sat there in a lotus position and laughed at all that was said. He was another freethinker, so free that he had lived with the girl for a few weeks, and then ran off when she tried getting into his bed. Maria one seemed a good-humoured type and just sat quietly looking out of the window into the passing night as the van sped along the highway on the road to surf, high adventure, and Caños de Mecca.

Then we started slowing and Maria one called out, '"La pasma."' (The old bill.) And then, '"Y a la mitad del camino, bajo las ramas de un olmo, Guardia Civil caminera.'" (And halfway down the track, below the branches of an elm, Guardia Civil suddenly appeared.)

Hey, I thought, I know that, we did it at school. Amazing, a girl who really loved poetry. And I completed the words from memory. The words of the incredible Spanish poet Lorca, from Granada. I had learnt it in French and the original Spanish. The professor had insisted we memorise it, as he said it was truly beautiful.

"'Lo llevo codo a codo. Antonio Torres Heredia, hijo y nieto de Camborios. Viene sin vara de mimbre, entre los cinco tricornios.'" (They arrested him elbow to elbow. Antonio Torres Heredia, son and grandson of Camborios. You come without your bamboo cane, encircled by five three-cornered hats.)

Maria looked at me, surprised, but with a smile. Looking out the window beside her, I recognised my Guardia Civil from San Lucar. Maria glanced at me, and seeing the sudden apprehension in my eyes, grabbed me and led me to the corner, behind the trio.

'Hay que esconderlo.' (He must be hidden.) She threw a blanket over me, and the trio moved backwards. The quiet dreamy girl had surprising authority in the group.

I could hear the civiles conversing with the driver.

'Un individuo muy peligroso, igual planea algunos ataques terroristas. Pero nada sí no lo habéis visto, seguir. La palabra de un hijo de civiles de casa cuartel nos vale.' (A very dangerous individual, he may be planning some terrorist attacks. But not to worry if you haven't seen him, continue. The word of the son of Civil Guards from family barracks is enough for us.)

'Hombre sí queréis podéis registrar atrás, como les he dicho, son chavales, estudiantes, que van de excursión.' (Gentlemen, if you wish, you may search in the back, although as I have told you, they are students on an excursion.)

'Con tu palabra nos vale.' (Your word is enough for us.)

The van started up again, and Maria came to uncover me. No one said anything, and she just looked at me.

"'¿Antonio, quien eres tu? Sí te llamaras Camborio, Hubieras hecho una fuente, de sangre con cinco chorros.'" (Antonio, who are you? If your name were Camborio, you would have created a fountain of blood with five spouts.)

She quoted Lorca with such vehemence and passion that I was swept up by the moment. The danger had passed, averted by her hand, and this incredible girl just sat there calmly quoting Garcia Lorca at me.

She looked into my eyes and I returned her look. We just sat there whilst all around was silent, the echoes of Lorca's words reverberating in our minds.

'Is it true what they said? Are you a criminal, a terrorist?'

I answered, 'No, in no way at all.'

She said, 'I know you're not. I just asked you for them,' she gestured around to include the others.

'Le tuve que esconder. A Lorca lo mataron porque era hermoso y homosexual, y porque sus palabras les asustaban, y porque tenían el poder. Mataron al Camborio porque era gitano y porque podían. Y yo no quería que le mataran a el.' (I had to hide him. They killed Lorca because he was beautiful and a homosexual and because his words frightened them, and because they had the power. They killed El Camborio because he was a gypsy and because they could. I didn't want them to kill him.)

Then the tears started to fall from her eyes, and Lanzarote was beside her in an instant, cradling her as he would a baby.

Ruben told me not to worry, that she was just very intense. He asked me why they were looking for me and I told him briefly what had happened at San Lucar. He said it all seemed very strange to him. Then the Toñi brigade started asking questions and Ruben worked wonders at fobbing them off. I noticed that when the marijuana joint was passed around, Ruben didn't smoke. And yet it was he who had originally spoken to me about buying some weed. I got the idea that he was an observer; he participated in what he wanted to, and no one was his peer. There was much more to Ruben than met the eye.

It wasn't long before the van left the main highway, and through the window, we began to get glimpses of the sea. The road wound through copses of fir trees and amongst wide areas of wild moorland, until suddenly we were driving alongside the shoreline and there were breakers, big Atlantic waves, starting maybe 150 metres offshore. Small figures on boards were cresting up their flanks, others rode the waves prostrate on their boards; some were riding standing upright, the more skilful zigzagging as they went or riding into the tube made by the wave as it rolled over onto itself. The early morning sun was shining from the east and the sea glittered with millions of darting fragments of brightly illuminated seawater catching its brilliant rays and reflecting them crazily, celebrating the birth of yet another day of marvellous creation. Everyone in the van was busying themselves donning swimsuits and short wetsuits and remarking on the waves.

'Que olas, tío, que olas.' (What waves, man, what waves.) Ruben pushed a small board and a wetsuit at me, which I hastily put on. Everyone leapt from the van as it came to a standstill. Boards under our arms, we rushed towards the sea. Plunging into the water, we swam, paddling towards the breakers and cutting through or going around them. The water felt cold but you hardly noticed it with the exhilaration that had invaded us. We waited in groups, floating in the calmer area where the breakers passed and grew, looking out for our waves to come. Then a big one built up, too far off for me, but Toñi, Lanzarote, and some others went with it. Someone was riding standing and going into the tunnel—it was big. Whoever it was moved around, finding the best positions in the heart of the wave and stayed with it all the way to the beach.

Ruben shouted, 'That was Toñi! Man, she can surf!'

Then a big one came right where we were and I paddled vigorously to stay with her till I got to just beyond her crest so that I was no longer powering, it was the wave that was carrying me forward. I got the feel of it at once, it was all a question of riding in just the exact spot, not too far forward nor too far back. I could feel the need for maintaining the right balance as the wave was holding me up and driving me forward; adrenaline rushed through me and I felt incredible. So with my instant confidence, I tried gingerly getting to my feet, kneeling first, then falteringly standing on wobbling legs. Suddenly, whoomph! The whole thing went and I was caught up in the wave, my board was wrenched from me. I was tumbling, seawater going up my nostrils; the sea was holding me under. I felt a spasm of panic; I just couldn't get to the surface and breathe, then just as suddenly, my unexpected ride was over. I found my feet, stood, and drank in the fresh delicious air. I looked around for my board and saw a bearded guy smiling my way. A guy with a face like, well, the archangel Gabriel. I mean, he just looked sort of ultra biblical. He wasn't that big, but his shoulders were wide and his face sort of radiated goodness, so I smiled back.

'I'm sorry, do I know you?'

He rumbled back, 'No,' and as a sort of afterthought, added, 'but you have met my family, poet.'

I knew who he was at once, he was our driver and probably Maria's brother.

'Maria is your sister? And you are the child from the Guardia Civil barracks?'

He smiled and sat down, shielding his eyes as he looked out to sea.

'Look, there she is, my little sister, another child of the waves. The only contact I have ever had with the Guardia Civil is being stopped for speeding. But I have the badge and look the part. And anyway, they weren't for real.

'My mother said to me, "Look out for her, Mahatma," so I am a camp follower, a groupie. With them, it's a sort of religion; they just follow waves. I know guys, and girls, but mainly guys who do only that. It's not as if the waves here are like in Hawaii, but these guys abandon everything, career and even family. It's true they seem really happy. Perhaps they know best, but when they get ill or old, it's mother or father or brother who must help. I, myself, am a catamaran type.'

'So am I. That's how I got here from Africa.'

'A big boat?'

'Fourteen footer.'

'You're a crazy kid.'

His name was Mahatma, and he told me that he knew the Guardia were not right as they had an unmarked car, one uniformed agent, one plainclothes, and they were not following procedure. Then he looked at me.

'You must know what it's about. These people have their protocols they always follow, yet this time…'

So I told him my story, and as I was finishing, Maria and Ruben came up the sand with Lanzarote. They collapsed, spent, on the sand around us. Mahatma said nothing, I supposed he was just an absorbing silent type.

We lay in the sun chatting, laughing, and talking surf. Someone brought bottles of water from the van. Once the surfers were rested, they began returning to the waves. I went with Maria and Ruben. We got out to beyond where the waves promised great things; this time, I hoped I could just stay on my feet. We waited, just paddling and laughing at Ruben's antics, waiting for a wave with our names on it. I missed a beauty, fooling about, but Ruben and Maria sailed off. I saw them go, slowly get to their feet, crouching down, and riding the wave to the shore. I saw a really nice one and paddled like mad to get onto it. Just a little further, and I was on its pivotal point, balancing so that the wave would drive me, but not too far forward so as to lose it. Holding the edges, I went up onto my right knee, getting my balance before trying the second foot, and then I was up, keeping my right foot ahead and the other behind and to the left, grimly keeping my balance. The wave went its course, and I reached the beach still standing, only losing momentum, causing the board to sink under my weight. They gave me a thumbs up, and I felt on top of the world. So we surfed and surfed till the waves started to lose their power with the onset of the evening and the influence of Mother Moon.

We all crashed onto the sand, totally exhausted, yet exhilarated and joyously happy. Everyone acknowledged me, and even Toñi gave me a beautiful fleeting smile. I felt so full, so complete, but inside me was a nagging, a voice in my head saying 'Don't forget your father, remember who you are.'

As the sun went down, sandwiches were produced and Mahatma began speaking, in a low voice, but one that could be heard by all. Maria had told me he was an encyclopaedia of useless but wonderful knowledge.

'¿Caños de Mecca era una pueblo de moda para tomar las aguas, un espa, en tiempos del Caliphato, sabéis?' (Did you know Caños de Mecca was a spa town noted for its waters in the time of the Caliphate?) He looked around. 'Los caños son chorros de agua dulce que se proyectan desde los acantilados, y que eran sagrados para los musulmanes.' (The caños are streams of fresh water which project from the cliff faces and were held sacred by the Muslim people, the people of the caliphates.)

'And where were the Spanish people at this time?' Ruben asked him in English, apparently for my benefit.

I spoke out, and they all looked at me. It seemed like a practised ritual; I was the new boy.

'The first invading Muslims did not dispossess the Spanish. They in fact battled with the Visigoths, who were just 2 percent of the population. The Spanish people were just as happy living under Muslim as Visigoth domination. The first invader was not an Arab, he was a Berber.

'He came in the name of the Arabs. He was a Berber general, Tariq Ibn Ziyad, leading his own people, just 7,000 troops, but he had sworn loyalty to Al-Walid Caliph of Damascus. He overran the whole peninsula, and the Arab armies that followed him a year later consolidated their rule. These were the Umayyad people.'

'But your people, Masuhun?'

'We were the race of Tariq Ibn Ziyad, although many of us were Christians dating back to the Romans, and others became Christian once in Spain.'

'And now, Masuhun, what are you?' Maria asked. 'What is your faith?' Again the question; again faith, how important it is to believe.

'I believe in God and in good. I am named for the Messias, Jesus of Nazareth. I believe fervently in a single God who watches over all people, and I accept all faith in a God to be the same, just in a different way. Some people would say that I am a religious eclectic.'

'What if I choose to worship the devil?' Eduardo spoke with a cynical leer etched faintly onto his darkening features.

I replied without thinking. 'Then you have chosen the road of evil, or perhaps it has chosen you, and you are weak. If you just jest, then do not, because there are powers of darkness you cannot begin to comprehend.'

He leapt to his feet and pointed fixedly at me, making it obvious it was not a conversation that he wanted. For some reason, he was challenging me and embarrassing most of the group.

To avoid any unpleasantness, I stood, said goodnight, went close to the van where Lanzarote and others were sleeping, and put my head down to sleep.

And again as I slept, regiments of knights wearing white tunics boldly emblazoned with red crosses marched under banners and metal crucifixes that glinted in the gleam of a sun long fading in the west. And marching towards them, mighty in their numbers, the proud unruly turbaned regiments of the great eastern prophet. But the clashes, which were innumerable, were of both great brotherhoods fighting vast evil looking serpents that emerged slithering from the ranks of both armies. And then I saw a fighter wielding his sword, slicing at the face of an enraged beast. I saw his face. It was Afra. It was my father. I must have screamed, as when I opened my eyes, Ruben, Maria, and the trio were there. Ruben was holding my arm.

'Una pesadilla, a nightmare. You screamed. You all right, man?'

I nodded and made my way towards the shore, wanting to be alone. I sat there for a while looking out to sea and at the moon, my agitation dissipating as rapidly as it had come. I wondered at the magnificence of creation and gave thanks. 'Thank you, my Lord, for every minute.' Or, as the Muslims say, 'Alhamdulilah.' Except that they say it with every second breath. Toñi sat down beside me.

'Do you remember your dreams? I do sometimes, especially my nightmares.'

I looked at her; she was incredibly sweet, perfect in every way.

'The word nightmare is thought to come from the incubus or succubus riding on your chest in the form of a mare, as you sleep.'

'Huh! All satanic and religious stuff was just fed to mankind and swallowed by all before the onset of science. But let's face it, in our new

enlightened world, it's all just gobbledygook. Hey, let's go up to this café
I know and get a snack.'

I protested my lack of funds, but my stomach rumbled loudly
just at that moment and we laughed.
'Don't worry, pay me back some other day,' she said, and I followed.

And the cock crowed again.

Toñi was just fourteen when her uncle raped her for the first time. It was statutorily a rape, although from a moral standpoint, it was another of those tiny undeclared battles in the war between men and women. It had been Pedro's undefined task to provide a shoulder for the solitary girl during the turbulent days of the divorce. Pedro could see in the girl a mirror image of her mother, the petulant hated torturer of his beloved brother Adrian.

He would spend many afternoons in the matrimonial home, alone with a child who had been destroyed emotionally by not only the lack of love, but the knowledge that her only value to either of her parents was as a bartering point or bone of contention. Pedro, young himself and wifeless, did his best to fill the gap. The beauty of the child and her natural coltish way of cavorting around began to arouse him in a way that was anathema to his Jesuit upbringing. It began one afternoon when she lay by him laughingly looking into his face as he attempted to read.

'Tienes la piel tan bonita,' (You have the loveliest skin,) she remarked.

He ignored her.

'Y los labios mas increíbles.' (And the most incredible lips.)

She kissed him, and he, lost and overcome by the young excited breathing of the child, pushed his tongue inside her mouth and felt the warmth and taste. She climbed astride him and pushed against his arousal. When she sensed his struggles to feel and caress her buttocks and breasts she pulled back saying, 'Later, perhaps. These things happen of their own accord.'

Admonished and thankful, it struck him just how like her mother she truly was. It was in fact her mother, Natasha, Pedro would have loved to take viciously and sodomise cruelly once she was spent. In fact, when younger, Natasha had taken an interest in the young man that had never been reciprocated. The girl, in spite of being only fourteen, a young hatchling, knew her power and how to use her claws.

The dilemma persisted in spite of his attempts through his brother to try to reach some sort of accommodation that would find a school or a governess for the child. Toñi, as all children her age in Spain, was equipped with all the technology, and so harassed him continuously, sending him suggestive photographs and promises of love. Finally one weekend, Pedro obligatorily succumbed. He arrived for the evening during the fortnight she spent with Adrian. Pedro had not even been able to protest; his brother had just sent him a phone message telling him to come home and subsequently disconnected his mobile. Pedro had convinced himself that she was a child, and if anything, just messed around with boys at school.

After a light supper, as they were watching a movie together, he sneaked off and locked himself into his room. It seemed like not a minute had passed before she knocked on his door.

'¿Pedro, porque me has dejado sola? No te he hecho nada hoy, seré buena te lo prometo.' (Pedro why have you left me on my own? I haven't done anything wrong today, I promise you I'll be good.)

He steeled himself, even when he heard her crying through the locked door. It was all so confusing; his instincts, his body yearned for her, and in reality this desire had been created by her, also instinctively. But her age said she was an innocent, and his morality and strict upbringing, as well as fear of the family scandal and legal consequences, stopped him from going anywhere with the girl. On the other hand, he felt sorry for her and her loneliness, as well as responsible, since she was in his care. He sometimes felt that he was babysitting a tiger. He tried to phone his brother, but got no answers to his multiple texts and calls. When she knocked again on his door and sobbingly told him that she would throw herself from the landing, he relented and opened the door to a weeping girl who came into his arms seeking comfort. So he rubbed her back and kissed her forehead, and she kissed him. He was lost again as she, having taken possession of his arousal with her searching hands, fumbled, undoing his trousers in spite of his feeble protestations. Then suddenly, the doorbell rang.

A boy from school, she said, she had just forgotten. They opened the door and a boy of about her age waved off the waiting car. Then he saw Pedro and stutteringly asked, '¿Quien es este?' (Who is this?)

To which she promptly answered, 'Es mi tío, Pedro.' (It's my uncle Pedro.) 'Olvide decirle que vendría a hacer los deberes conmigo.' (I forgot to tell him you would come to do your homework with me.) 'Es Matías.' (This is Mathias.)

The kid muttered a hello, and she said, 'Vamos.' They went to her room, where she turned and smiled at Pedro brightly, then proceeded to close and lock the door. What went on, he really could not say. He should have been delighted, but in fact he felt viciously jealous. He cursed himself for feeling what should have been the last thing for him to feel in the circumstances. He just kept thinking that she was now doing to the kid what she would have done to him, and then he wondered at this impromptu arrangement with the boy and whether she had engineered it to make him feel jealous. He thought lots of things, and more than once stopped himself going and rapping on the door. Several hours of torture went by until at last the doorbell went, and the boy's father carted him off.

Pedro sat in silence in the lounge and she went to her room. Eventually, she tiptoed in, in her nightgown, turned on the TV, and sat there watching it. He had managed to completely neutralise his mind and really just didn't care.

Then she said, 'Solo es un crio.' (He's just a little kid.)

He studiously ignored her and fought vainly to understand the words he was reading,

'Estoy tan liada, Pedro. Igual me debes castigar, azotarme.' (I'm just so confused, Pedro. Perhaps you should just punish me, spank me.)

'¿Por que motivo?' (Whatever for?) he asked her impatiently.

'Solo porque tu lo deseas, y yo por razones, me lo merezco.' (Just because you want to, and I, for whatever reason, deserve it.) With that, she shed her nightgown and was over his knee in a flash, her beautiful young naked body draped tantalizingly, tender white buttock cheeks awaiting his sentence. So he beat her, and soundly, and after, she gathered her robe and went to her room sniffling silently.

He managed to stay away for several weeks, giving excuses such as exams, illness, commitments with friends.

Adrian was often onto him, 'Macho! Macho!' he would stridently call his brother. '¿Que pasa contigo? Sabes que la niña esta loca para verte.' (What's the matter with you, you know the girl is crazy to see you.) Thoughts of her tiny breasts, nipples hard with her unsated desire, the musky odour of mad but delicious lust, and her stunning soft warm little round buttocks there over his knees flashed through his mind.

'Adrian, I am really so busy, what with exams.'

Hushing him, Adrian reminded him, with the scantiest delicacy, of things past. Of boarding school days when he would stand up with absolutely no reservation to whomever or whatever may have come along to upset his younger sibling. To taking his brother with him, in spite of his various friend's many protestations, to every event, in order to avert the child from brooding upon his parents' constant and overlong absences.

'I really would be with her all the time, but Natasha is trying to destroy me and I must fight. It's as if she were engineering it so that I couldn't be with Toñi. When I mention to her in the midst of a yelling match that the child finishes up with you so many days and nights, she seems to go all quiet, even smug, as if…' he trailed off. 'I don't know…'

Pedro, desperate to escape returning to the house, faked an accident and finished up with a truly broken ankle. His plan totally backfired. Even in the hospital, with his leg slung up and in plaster, she found her way to be alone by his bedside.

'Sí, Hermana, lo comprendo, no son horas de visita. Me echare como una ratoncita en el sofá. Claro, sí, os necesitamos, el timbre.' (Yes, sister I understand, it's not visiting hours. I'll just lie down here like a little mouse on the sofa. Yes, of course, if we need you, the bell.) She tells them he's her favourite uncle. And the family are so influential that in spite of his attempts to protest, they see only her side of it.

'Hermana, no es para nada necesario que la niña se quede. Yo debo descansar para recuperarme.' (Sister, it's not at all necessary that the child stays. I should really rest to recover.)
But his words seem to evaporate; people just didn't listen.

'No se preocupe vd Señor Pedro. Es solo una niña y no molesta,' (Don't you worry, Señor Pedro. She is only a child and will give no trouble.) Then, looking at Toñi fondly, again, 'No molesta ella. Es muy guapa.' (She doesn't trouble anyone. She's a very pretty child.)

So Pedro just laid back, stunned and apprehensive. Yet his body, in spite of his ills, was already responding to Toñi's presence, something he would have believed impossible. Once they were alone, she told him she was sorry, and that the spanking had been good for her, that she had been bad to him. He asked her how her mother allowed her to come and stay at the hospital.

'She brought me here,' she said, looking at him from beneath raised eyebrows, as if to see his reaction.

Pedro hid his consternation. It began to dawn on him that perhaps Natasha knew everything, that maybe she was the architect of the whole mess. The girl kissed him and he tried to wriggle away, but was hampered by his suspended leg. He felt her warm hand enter his pyjamas, and the extent of her passion as her lips moved to the most intimate areas of his body. He didn't protest. He was confused and angry, but whatever he may ever have said, he was guilty from the very first kiss, that day when he was reading. He should have complained, stopped it at the very start. But in feminist Spain, he would have been guilty even if he had never kissed her, just by being in the same house as the child, and they would destroy him. Anyway, most of the judges were female as well.

So he just laid back and let it happen; he let her devour him again and again.

The next time, once fully recovered, he went to spend a night at their house, Toñi was in a diffident, strange mood.

The following day, his world crashed around him when the Policia Nacional came to his house in force to arrest him for the indecent assault and rape of a minor. As things unfolded, it transpired that his case was lost, as they had produced semen stained sheets and underclothes off the girl's bed. To protest that she had deviously collected it when she was assaulting him as he lay inert in the hospital would have convinced nobody. Pedro's lawyers tried to establish that the girl was no novice to sexual relations, as Spanish law was more concerned with the sexual age of the girl than her physical age. But on the stand, Toñi turned out to be a consummate actress, and his cause was lost.

Pedro often had the idea that the whole thing had been engineered by mother and daughter to get at his brother, Adrian.

'You would need to be really evil to manipulate your daughter in such a way,' Adrian opined.

'It's not the mother who did the manipulating,' Pedro replied. 'I think it was the girl. I think she is especially bad, evil. Think of it Adrian, she is the child of a Spanish man and Russian girl about whom we really know very little, only that she has always been as rich as Croesus. Think of all that went on in Russia for all those years, and that it wasn't the simple God-fearing folk that became rich in the collapse of the Soviet and the rise of the new order. These people are different from us, so different you can't imagine.'

'Perhaps I can,' groaned Adrian. 'Perhaps I already know it.'

Three years later, Toñi's mother Natasha died in an accident, and Toñi, just eighteen, inherited a vast fortune. The circumstances of her mother's demise were unclear, but the family's pressure ensured that the case was rapidly filed away and forgotten. Toñi moved to an enormous rural family estate in the south of Spain but lived a very normal, even frugal, lifestyle, as if she didn't want to miss living a real life by surrounding herself with the trappings of wealth. There was a maturity to her thinking that alienated even the most persistent relative in their efforts to guide her. She brought boys home and girls, and some stayed to live. Rumours developed in the village about drugs and drink and orgies, and even a homeless vagabond who was killed in the area. When questioned about things, Toñi would shrug her shoulders and chalk it all up to envy of the big estate, rich heiress, and extravagant friends; all that one would expect. The one aspect of her life that was not frugal was in buying expensive toys for her girlfriends and boyfriends. Rolexes and the latest, best tablets and sports cars, clothes, mobile phones, but never cash. Rapidly, they grew to depend on her whims.

Juan and Eduardo had convinced her to go surfing, so they latched onto some people they knew and set off, the threesome and Maria. Toñi was hit as if by a thunderbolt when Masuhun came into the van. She saw him, with his fresh uprightness, his apparent honesty and decency, and she was amused, but somehow, even in the dark, he made her heart pound. As the day dawned with its inherent enhanced visibility, she realised he was beautiful. His easy smile, locks of thick black rich hair falling in natural loose ringlets towards his strong shoulders, lithe, slim, catlike body with a hint of a cheeky upturned behind. But it was not just the beauty that moved her. She was in turmoil; something primeval inside her was telling her to hate him, to obliterate him, like that holy traveller, that filthy tramp they had set on fire. She wanted him, to own him, taste him, punish him, subjugate him, and eventually destroy him. To wipe that smirk of godliness off his face. But in her perversity, she also wanted him to love her, to possess her violently, dominate her. Faith? He was going to need mountains of faith to continue believing once she was done with him.

I followed her off the beach. She wore a long Moroccan silk gown embroidered with gold thread all along the edges. It was a creamy colour and hung open with only a red silk scarf tied around her waist to hug it to her lithe body. Her skin, where the sun had not toasted it, was milky white. She had removed her bikini top for the night it seemed, and as I had startled her with my nightmare, she was still dressed for bed, so to speak. The effect was quite non-plussing. Her breasts, firm and youthful, filled out the flimsy robe. Below the waist, her beautiful young girl thighs tapered down from apparent nudity, the gown creating the illusion that she was naked beneath its luxurious caress. On her feet, she wore hand-painted Moroccan leather slippers that flapped ever so indistinctly as she walked. She looked into my eyes with her smiling blues ones, took my hand and wrapped my arm around her, bringing her face closer to mine. I could feel her nipples brush my chest. I could feel her warmth and smell her young, clean, salty odour. Then with a giggle, she unwound herself, spinning out of my grasp, and ran off down the street, leaving me to chase after her.

The café, Su Primo Su Hermano, was packed with young people. It seemed as if space was magically cleared for us as we passed through. She turned many heads when we walked in, not surprisingly.

The noise level 'Is crazy,' she said at once.

For me, even though I didn't object, it was horrendous. We went out and found a table with white sofas around it just sitting empty like an oasis in the desert. Every other table and all the chairs were taken, and people were standing around holding their drinks and conversing, shouting to be heard above the racket. A girl asked us what we would like, I asked for limeade made from Abu Dhabi limes with lots of ice, but as she just looked at me, I looked at Toñi. Toñi wanted gazpacho with vodka, so I had the same without alcohol. I would have preferred the limes, off trees on the edge of the desert in Abu Dhabi. They would be collected when made brittle by the heat, then crushed and mixed with water and honey to make limeade, which was truly an elixir from the gods. But when in Spain, so I asked Toñi what it was exactly that we had ordered.

'Tomato, cucumber, capsicum, all in the mixer with a bit of dry bread. Lemon and olive oil, salt, and the magical ingredient that only I use, cumin.'

She sat opposite me suddenly coy and ladylike, explaining the secrets of Spanish cuisine. The gazpacho came and I drank mine down with delight. It was incredible, I could taste everything, even the cumin; it was so cold and so wonderful. The music still blasted. Everyone appeared drunk or drugged or something and seemed to have his or her mobile phone in hand.

'Why are so many people engrossed with their phones,' I asked, quite bemused.

'Jaja, that's how they communicate. Most will stay all night, get drunk or stoned, and text each other. I don't think people have fun really. They pretend to enjoy themselves, and the boys all hope to get laid and the girls sit back on their hands, look around, and decide whether it's a boy or girl for the night. The ones who have a home to go to—many are children of broken homes—still escape in groups and totter back home waking up the whole town on their way, just to show how macho they are. The less attractive girls do the same in gangs, swearing, urinating, and getting up to all sorts of trouble as they go. But their phones, their phones are their magic carpets. With them, they can message unseen or out of sight friends and regale them with stories of their incredible night. They can even phone each other and talk about the boy or girl they nearly seduced, and do you know? Everyone believes everything; even they themselves learn to believe their own fantasies. And the good-looking sexy girls, they all want the same boys, and when and if they get him, they drop him to keep on top, like their modern feminist mummy has brainwashed them to do. And if she ever falls in love, it's normally with the biggest chulo. Now, Spanish women hate men who are chulo, unless it's her son or the guy she's in lust for. He has to be the biggest chulo ever.'

It seemed to me that she was full of contradictions, but then perhaps she was just talking about different types of girls?

'And what about you, Toñi, who are you in this world?'

'I am one of the girls who sit on their hands but have yet to decide on the right boy. I don't know, there are many things other than sex.'

'No, no way are you like these girls. There's a worldliness about you. I only know you, well I don't know you at all, and yet I get a vibe.'

'Well for one thing, I can think. I can string a bunch of words together as I just did. If I try to converse with these kids, well, I'm not being nasty, but it seems that the great majority of today's youth, here anyway, are losing the gift of articulate speech.

'But you asked about me. I'm a romantic, I believe in love. Once you find your other half, you should love him or her with all your heart.'

We just sat for a while, drinking gazpacho and eating plates of paella.

'How come your English is so good?'

'I went to a private English school, and had English governesses.'

'I've seen European movies with governesses, and –'

She cut me short. 'The families are rich, is that what you're asking? Well I don't have a family, so you needn't worry, and yes we were rich,' She stood up from the sofa where she had been sitting and I could see tears glistening in her eyes. She looked around wildly as if deciding where to go, then she visibly relaxed and came and sat beside me. 'I'm so alone now.'

So I caressed her hair and rubbed her back as I would do to my sister, and I felt the warm tears coursing down my face as she found comfort in my embrace. I wondered what had upset her.

A tall, striking, dark-skinned guy arrived and sat on one of our sofas. The music changed to Spanish flamenco ballads, and the new guy across the table spoke. '¿Y ese tío?' He looked only at her, '¿Quien es? Payo no es.' (And that guy? Who is he? He's not European. Meaning he could be a gipsy.)

'Es un amigo, Ingles.' (He's an English friend.)

He looked at me, and I could see he was drunk or drugged. I smiled at him.

'What you want here, guy? This is my sofa, my bar—the girl is mine too.' She just sat there expressionless and quiet, so I did the same. The man was getting nervous and aggressive, and he kicked the table.

I looked at Toñi. This was not my serpent, and I could not see myself in shining armour. My battles, the ones the old lady had described, were other than just a barracks skirmish. So I wanted to just go. 'Let's go back,' I said.

She just looked at me, and he said, 'You go, English. Fuck off, bastard.'

I stood up and reached out for the girl's hand, firmly pulling her up with me. 'Better go. The tribes are gathering,' I said with an attempt at humour, but they actually were gathering. Three or four young friends of his had joined him. As we walked around the sofa, he kicked the table at me.

He stood up, shrugging off the guys around him, 'A este lo dejo frio.' (This one I will leave cold.)

He came up behind me and pushed me with both hands, grabbing my shoulders.

I twisted round, trapping his extended right arm under my armpit. I grabbed his wrist and twisted it viciously. He was bent over to avoid my breaking his wrist, so I heel kicked him in the butt firmly towards the table, which he took right in the face.

We ran, she laughing loudly, and then as we turned the corner, a big Mercedes four by four came speeding towards us. The door opened and I grabbed her hand to run the other way, but she pulled back. 'It's our car, come on.' By then Eduardo had jumped out. He just stood waiting, apparently for a couple of the guys who were still chasing us. He waved them towards his chest as if inviting them to come at him, but they ran off. Perhaps they knew something I didn't. So Toñi and I jumped into the car. Juan was at the wheel and Maria two sat curled up in a seat, asleep.

'Venga, Eduardo. Móntate ya que nos vamos.' (Come on, Eduardo. Get in, we're going.)

He came to the car, kicking it and slamming the door viciously.

'¿Donde fuisteis? ¡Coño!' (Where did you go? Shit!) It seemed that he was madder with us than with our pursuers.

Toñi sat in the front seat with me and Juan. She just ignored Eduardo, who sat fuming in the back.

'No vea como le ha dao al Marco, el Masuhun,' (You should have seen how Masuhun sorted out that Marco) she laughed loudly.

'Es peligroso ese muchacho,' (That young man is dangerous) said Juan.

'Un puto payaso,' (A bloody clown) said Eduardo.
'Peligrosa soy yo,' (I am dangerous) she cut in, laughing again. 'O no?' (Or not)

They didn't answer her.

Juan spoke to me. 'Mahatma, Ruben, Maria, all go home. They look you, you not here, so they go,' he explained in his rough English. I gave him a thumbs up, and he smiled.

'Gracias, Juan, but where can I find them?'

'Don't worry, tío. You can stay with us.' He looked towards Toñi, who smiled. 'Otro día you see Mahatma.'

I was in no mood for going against the grain, so I just nodded and smiled at them both.

'Where are we going?' I asked Juan.

'Medina Sidonia, where Toñi lives,' he giggled. 'We all live there. I am from there, mozzer and papa. It's on a mountain, view of bahia, sea. Eduardo, he is from Ronda.'
He looked back towards where Eduardo sat morosely.

'Eduardo is quiet person. No talk, just do, like verdugo (executioner),' he giggled and made a head chopping motion. He drove slowly, as if enjoying the scenery, although it was dark. Toñi was sitting snuggled up against my back. I didn't dare move, as I didn't want to disturb her. We drove on through the night till at last we stopped before a big gate with a majestic overhead arch. The gates swung back noiselessly and the Mercedes purred in and onto a cement driveway. It seemed endless, till at last, a forecourt overhung by an enormous metal trellis loaded with vines, loomed. We drove under it and up towards a large hacienda style house.

I gently woke her, and we all traipsed into the house, where everyone made off to their own quarters. She led me by the hand to a room, handed me a towel, gave me a kiss, and went out, closing the door behind her.

I lay down for a minute to try the bed and fell into a deep sleep. Later, refreshed, I explored the room and found some clothes and a bathroom. The floor was laid in a sort of Arabic style, with terracotta tiling set off with wood edging. The décor or feel of the room was, I imagined, sort of Andalusian, dating back, in ways, to the days of the caliphates. Two big French windows, draped with heavy curtains, likely opened onto some sort of terrace. I pulled one of the curtains back and opened the windows to let in some air. There were green blinds made of slatted wood which I also unfastened and pushed open. A creeper of some sort that hung quite densely over the windows exuded a fragrant and pleasing scent, probably jasmine. Outside, a balcony seemed to run all around the courtyard where we had left the car. Then I saw her from the corner of my eye, the movement close by, no more than some eight metres. She was grasping the wrought ironwork of the balcony of the room next to my own. It was Maria two, and she was completely naked. I knew she could not see me through the jasmine. I watched and found her body very pleasing. It did not occur to me that I was acting as a voyeur and had no permission to observe her. But I was entranced, unthinking. Ever since I had first seen her I had noticed, albeit innocently, the shape of her body in her high cut jeans shorts and tight little bodice. And now she was here. Her buttocks were soft yet firm and just right, sensual and beautiful. Her cheeks seemed to cling together briefly as she moved, stretching, arcing her body first one way and then kicking out a leg and opening both, sinking down till it seemed she would split in two. But seconds later, I was startled out of my reverie as a man, also naked, joined her, clutching her by the shoulders, and in rhythm with her movement, slowly taking command. Guiding her to the railing, he bent her body over, exposing her sweet white buttocks to what I suddenly noticed was his very erect penis. I watched mesmerised as he penetrated her time and again, driving in first the tip and slowly, an ever increasing length, while her cried echoed louder and louder around the veranda. I realised that he was not taking her in a normal way, he was taking her anally. I suddenly also realised that I was swollen and engorged, excited by the spectacle, so I turned away to close the windows and curtains. I had just tasted what in the west is so freely available, pornography. I felt confused, attracted on the one hand and dismayed with myself on the other for watching, and wanting to watch. What was right and what wrong? I knelt and asked the mother and Jesus to guide me.

So I lived day after day in that beautiful hacienda, and slowly I saw what life was to its inhabitants. You never saw the staff; they must have been trained to be ghostlike. The only evidence I ever saw of them was the way the house was maintained in impeccable order, and of course the maid I saw reflected in a mirror, but when I looked behind me she had gone. Disappeared like a spectre in a movement of air and a silently closing door.

There was also a little old gardener, wizened and dwarf like who, whenever he saw me wandering alone through the beautiful gardens, beckoned me secretively with great urgency etched on his face and say, '¡Vete de aquí! ¡Vete! Solo hay demonios, vete mientras puedas, tú no eres de ellos. ¡Vete!' (Go from here! Go! There are only demons here, go whilst you can, you are not one of them. Go!)

I asked him about the different plants and flowers, and he was delighted to explain. We became friends, and he employed me weeding flowerbeds and pruning trees. He called me from where I was trundling a barrowful of manure one morning to help him, and together we grafted the branches of orange trees onto sterile lemon trees, and onto crab orange trees, bearers of the bitterest of fruit. If the grafts took successfully, he told me, we would be responsible for so many wonderful oranges. His name was Richa, actually Richard. In fact, his real name was Juan, but many years ago a movie came to his mother's pueblo and they saw Richard Widmark acting, and from that day on he was Richa. So I took to getting up early and helping Richa. Like with Amador, we didn't speak much, although my Spanish was improving, and there were always signs to fall back on. There just didn't seem a need for words, just a constant steady toil, turning soil, pruning, cleaning out flowerbeds.

Toñi courted me patiently, using her wiles as a woman to arouse my basic instincts, the kind that in my world should exist and be part only of the life of a man and his wife, or in the most extreme cases, of a young and intense love that had flowered and matured a little over at least a year or two of its existence. So I was able, by praying, to keep such desires and lustings at bay. She was also adamant that I should learn about computers and the internet, and so we spent part of each day playing with a world that, again, I did not want to be a part of. I could see aspects of this new science which could be useful to me in life, but it soon became apparent that the new technologies were completely taking over the existence of their users. She told me there were their billions of users all over the globe.

I understood that this and other technologies that were part of the new age and of human progress were here to stay. The betterment of the lot of humankind was at hand through them, but as I, with the eye of a newcomer, began to be aware of how they were being used, and to the ultimate benefit of whom, I felt disappointed, even betrayed. It seemed to me that people in this world were just accepting what was happening as unchangeable; that people had given up hope. And the irony was that the information I was gleaning to form these conclusions was coming off the web itself. So the knowledge of what was happening was there, the chinks in the armour were happening with Wikileaks, Snowden, Sauvage, and Moore, to name but a few. It would only take an idea or set of ideas, and their successful implantation in people's minds would start to change. But it would need to be powerful enough and go back to the rudimentary structures of our societies.

The other inhabitants of the hacienda, Eduardo, Maria, Juan, and Claudio, spent their days on their computers or mobile phones. That was their life. Willing victims? Or, worse, it was bred into them so they were an intrinsic part of it, the messages and lifestyle forming them whilst the world at large was subliminally brainwashed into accepting all the changes? They took the occasional break to eat or drink or attend to bodily functions. A bit like butterflies going from spot to spot as it grabbed their attention, They reacted to stimulants, technological and psychological in the main, or physical and readily at hand as they made themselves available or, as they desired, just took them. I knew that lots of physical intercourse of all sorts was going on between everybody. For one thing, my evening's entertainment of that first night reappeared, but this time with Juan and Eduardo as the actors. I immediately closed the windows and curtains. Perhaps I was just suspicious, but I wondered if it had all been staged for me, starting with Maria and Eduardo.

Toñi bought me things all the time, tablets and computers and a state of the art mobile phone for which I had little use. She gave me money, bought me new clothes, and slowly, she played her game of interest and disinterest, of good girl and bad girl. And I, not being made of steel, went along partially with her play and participated in the childish romping around, races, and breathless kissing that are parts of adolescent love. Looking back, I think that Toñi, or at least a part of her, really did fall in love with me. But there was always something brooding in my mind, telling me that things were not right and that the little old gardener, Richa, was right in warning me.

Then one night, she came to me as I slept. I awoke to find this wondrously beautiful girl naked in my bed. I could feel her warmth against my skin as her soft, young girl lips, mouth, and tongue explored my face. I was still drowsy, and it was like a sensual dream. I was totally aroused and her hands took all of me and caressed me. She moved down my body, hungrily kissing and eating me. I was in her mouth and it was total ecstasy. But then the vision of a serpent flitted across my mind, and my father, and the fact that this was not right. I gently took her head in my hands and moved her away. She kissed me, and would not stop, so I jumped out of bed and put on my jeans and shirt and ran out of the door. It wasn't that I did not want her, I did, so very much. I hardly knew her though, and we weren't man and wife; there wasn't even love. No, it wasn't right, but I felt so broken up.

So I walked for a while and then returned to my room, gathered up my few belongings, and left. For where, I knew not.

Rather than head for the highway I turned towards the backdrop of hills. I needed time to think, so I walked along a dirt track for what must have been hours. I heard a faint sound of water flowing and discovered a brook, from which I drank deeply. Sitting on a rock, I pondered whether I was being stupid. Perhaps if I went back, she would have gotten the message and leave me alone. It wasn't really her that worried me though, It was me; to stay with her was all so easy and beautiful. But I remembered the old woman's words, 'You, Masuhun, are chosen to follow the road of reason, find your way, and teach others to build a new truth.' To stay there with the girl wasn't right, in a place where there was no spirituality, constant displays of fornication to tempt me, people addicted to computers and social networks, and gifts, easily acquired goods for idle consumption. No, it was a trap; the old woman said that I would see evil, and I would be armed to recognise it. Good thing I didn't decide to settle in this country, I would have spent my every day discovering evil.

I heard a rustling in the bushes behind me and spun round. They leapt out so unexpectedly, and set upon me. I could feel brutal punches, cowardly blows, kicks, and what must have been a stick or a cudgel striking my legs and arms. I was so dizzy, I couldn't scream. I had fallen; they had beaten me to the ground. I didn't know what to do. I couldn't move anything, only my head, looking for help, which I knew would not come. My nose was hurting me. It was broken, and the blood from my nose and the rest of my wounds formed a puddle under my face.

I smelled urine; they had pissed on me. They wanted to grab my belt and take off my jeans, but I kicked out wildly, as this, this I didn't want them to do. I knew what they were after, they wanted to completely humiliate me and satisfy their own bestial appetites. Suddenly, it flashed into my head, an image of the Mother, and before her my father, dressed as before in a white tunic and wielding a mighty sword.

'Venga maricon mierda levanta.' (Come on you shit queer, get up) Up to that point I had been petrified, totally incapable of moving; my hands, and all of me, trembled. But I was not like them, the Mother and her Son were with me, along with my father, Afra, and I had a mission. A piece of rock was below my hand. I grabbed it, and with a superhuman effort, sprang to my feet screaming.

'Nooooooooooooooooooooooooo!'

I went for the closest one fearlessly; fury had armed me with total abandon. I sliced at his head, and the other two took to their heels as his blood spurted angrily over them. Did I kill him? Did I rape him? No, I was not like them. He lay there in his own blood, and I pulled off his hood. It was Eduardo.

The adrenaline spent, I felt so weak, and dropped to my knees. Richa suddenly appeared muttering and waving his hands at me. I knew what he was saying, that I hadn't listened to him. He leaned me on his back as much as he could and took me. We seemed to stumble for ages till, below a heavily overgrown part of the river bed, he showed me into a cave hidden by the dense foliage. He manoeuvred me in, where I collapsed and passed out.

The cave.

I came to, awakened by the shrill ringing of my telephone. I was in pain all over, in some places a dull aching and in others it was agony just to move. There was dried and caked blood all over me. I put my hand up to my face. My nose was twisted, broken, and my eyes badly swollen. I just lay there and silently said a prayer of thanks to the mother and her son for keeping me alive. But I also implored them to help me. Then I fell back into pain-racked sleep.

In my dream, an old woman tended me. She was thorough but ever so gentle, rubbing salves into my muscles, creams into my wounds, and washing the most intimate parts of me, which were also bruised, with infinite compassion and tenderness. She had me drink from a sponge. I could not see her, as she had placed something soothing over my very swollen eyes. One of my arms between elbow and wrist was twisted and probably broken, and she made a splint for it. Before setting the bone, she put a phial of liquid to my lips, and then I knew no more.

I had the other dream repeatedly, where the armies of the white cross-emblazoned tunics met the turbaned ranks and cavalry of the followers of the prophet from the east. But in their meeting, no blood was spilt between them, only the yellow blood of the hideous serpents that emerged from their very ranks.

But the dream of the old woman also kept returning, I could feel her love and her caring through her very touch, and in my dream, my wounded body left the ground and hung suspended on gentle cushions of the softest down.

Then one day, Richa woke me. I blinked and held my arm in front of my face to shield it from the early rays of morning sunlight that penetrated into my sanctuary.

'No pude venir antes. Te traigo comida y una manta por sí hace frio. Tienes buena pinta, y ni hueles mal ¿Oye y el brazo roto?' (I couldn't come any sooner. I've brought you food and a blanket for if it gets cold. You look good, you don't even smell bad. Hey and what about your broken arm?) He took my arm, the broken one, and I winced in anticipation, but there was no pain.

'¿Te duele? ¿Como que esta recto, normal? Estaba doblado, yo quise enderezártele y no podía porque gritabas. ¿Te duele o no? ¿Que no, y como se explica uno esto?' (Does it hurt? How come it's straight, normal? It was broken, twisted, I wanted to straighten it for you but couldn't because you kept screaming. Does it hurt or no? No? Then how do you explain this?)

I felt my arm and then ran a tentative hand over the rest of my body, seeking abrasions, wounds, or even painful areas, but there were none. It was true, what he was saying. I had come to the cave in a bad state, and just like that, all my pains and ailments had vanished. Perhaps it was natural, like the wounded soldiers who were cured by the penicillin in the soil they lay in. To say it was divine was pushing it; maybe the healing was psychosomatic and my credulous subconscious had speeded up the natural healing process. I thought I would put it to Richa, to see how he reacted.

'No se. En mis sueños había una vieja, ella venia cuando yo dormía, me sano las heridas, me lavo el cuerpo y me arreglo el brazo, pero solo fue un sueño.' (I don't know. In my dreams there was an old lady, she came when I was sleeping and cured my wounds, she washed my body and healed my arm, but it was just a dream.)

I said it haltingly, although I was still wondering if it were just my robust Berber constitution. But in the dream, she had been so real, and I was definitely better; and my broken arm had just gone and healed itself.

Richa made the sign of the cross.

'Ave María Santísima. Pero sí yo no creo en estas cosas, pero esto, esto me pone los pelos de punta. Y me dice el niño que solo fue un sueño. Niño, tu, seria un sueño, pero la señora te sano. Esto es obra de la virgen, parece que ella te sonríe.' (Hail to The Blessed Virgin. But I don't believe in these things, this makes my hair stand on end. And the boy tells me that it was just a dream. Boy, you, this may have been a dream, but the lady cured you. This is the work of the Virgin, she seems to smile on you.)

I was taken aback. This humble little man believed, in fact his faith was his reality, he tried to push it away, but he believed. But then again, perhaps it was in him, just bred into him as was the fatalism bred into the Muslim people, and a traditional unswerving faith in effigies of Virgin and child into the Catholics. But I, I who had now more than once been saved by their divine intervention, still did not have the strength to believe. I remembered a story in the New Testament where a centurion whose child was possessed said to Jesus, 'Lord I believe, help me to rid myself of my disbelief.' From that moment onwards, I decided that they were leading me by the hand. That I could do and undo, choose my path, evaluate good and bad, and in so doing, construct my truth, and they would be there for me when the trials and tribulations came my way, as I was sure they would.

'¿Que tiempo llevo dormido Richa?' (How long have I been sleeping, Richa?)

'Tres días. Pero, no pude venir, me seguían. Te buscan la Policía, los civiles, dicen que mataste al joven amigo de la Toñi con un navajazo.' (Three days. I couldn't come, they were following me. The police are looking for you, the Guardia Civil, they say you killed Toñi's young friend with a knife.)

'Pero sí yo solo me defendía, además no llevaba navaja.' (But I only defended myself, and anyway I had no knife.)

'Yo lo se, hijo. Cuando yo vine a buscarte no vi nada de heridas ni navajas, eso es esa chica tan mala que lo ha matado, como mato al otro hombre. Sigo en esa casa trabajando porque no me queda mas remedio. Además llevo cuidando esos jardines desde niño, y les tengo cariño. Pues yo me voy que sí no, me hechan de menos. Venga, ya volvere.' (I know it, son. When I arrived I saw no wounds or knives, that's the girl, the evil one who has killed him. She also killed that other man. I continue working in that house because I have no alternative. And anyway I have tended those gardens since I was a boy and I have lots of affection for them. Well, I'm off, otherwise they'll miss me. OK, I'll be back soon.)

I slept again till the phone, which had amazingly survived the beating I had received, rang again.
I answered it and kept silent.
'Masuhun, it's me, Toñi. Where are you? Are you all right? Baby, I know you're there. I love you, Masuhun. I want you to be with me. I will clear your name. You will be rich, most of the lands in the province are mine, all you can see is mine, and if you come to me and be mine all that which I possess will be yours also. Masuhun, listen to me. We will be enchanted and grow ever more wealthy whilst humanity withers around us. Masuhun, when this planet starts to die, we will have homes and wealth and power on other planets, we and our children. Masuhun, come to me. I love you.'

Again, the old woman in the sanctuary had warned me, 'They will seek to harm you and speak evil of you, because you believe.' So I answered her by restating my faith, 'Our father, who art in heaven,' I began, and at once I could hear spitting and the filthiest language I had ever heard. Then she started threatening abusively.

'Begone, satan,' I shouted and ended the call.

I knew she would continue to call me, and so I smashed the state of the art telephone against a rock. It was also my declaration of total separation from a world where people could only relate through technology, thereby relinquishing control of their lives to people and organisations they did not personally know. I had just come from a life sheltered from such things, but one would hardly need to be very intelligent to see what was happening.

The days went by and I recovered my strength. I would bathe my body often in the stream, the water so fresh and clean that I felt cleansed in not just body, but also in my spirit and my mind. The food was gone, but an afternoon of foraging in the woods behind my cave kept me fed. There were fig trees laden with big juicy black figs that I would wash in the river and eat whole, peel and all. Wild apples and almond trees were everywhere. The almonds were still young and in a gelatinous state, but wonderful to eat once you had battled with the shell that contained them. I walked naked much of the time to try and conserve my clothes, as they were the only ones I had. I grew brown and hard. My muscles were developing and I seemed to be slimmer but increasing in girth, all attributable to a fifteen-year-old man going on sixteen and living in nature.

It had its unwanted aspects also. At night, I kept having visions of naked bodies entering my head unbidden. I would grow stiff and could feel my testicles swell. Then I would see her lying there in ecstasy waiting for my manhood to enter into her. I would touch myself and become even more excited until I realised it was her, in my mind. So I would pray and ask for guidance and the thoughts would go. I came to understand why the monks of old used to practice self-flagellation. It was all too easy to develop an awareness of one's own body and an unnatural love of self when living alone.

One night they came. I could hear them long before they arrived. They had dogs by the sound of it, as I could hear the barking and the baying. For a moment I froze, petrified, my habitual fear taking hold of me. Then I knew what I needed to do. I dressed hurriedly, walked into the water, and set off upstream. I heard the noise of the breaking underbrush and the dogs, as well as the shouting of the men to my left, so I climbed onto the bank on my right and continued upstream. After that, I kept walking, alternating time in the stream and time on the bank. I had seen it in a movie once; that way the dogs would keep losing my scent, if indeed they had ever picked it up at all. It was quite obvious that the forces of law and order pursuing me had never seen the movie. They were probably too busy watching football.

As night fell, under the light of a full moon, I made my way back to my cave. It was the unlikeliest place for them to search, as they had already swept the area. I listened as I approached for any sound, the slightest hint of anything wrong, and I would have been off like a shot. But it was all quiet at my sanctuary, with the moon shining on the rippling water of the brook. I felt a little sentimental; after all, it had been my home for a few days.

Then, like a flash, I remembered the blanket. I had forgotten it. If they had stumbled on the cave, they would find it, know it was my lair, and if they were not entirely stupid, wait for me there. So I moved further away, to a position from which I could silently and rapidly retrace my steps and get away. I lay down against a tree and waited. I calculated that given that they were such a noisy bunch, it wouldn't be too long before they gave up and broke the silence, if they were there at all.

As I lay there, I realised the enormity of the situation. This was a manhunt, and I was the pursued, a murder suspect.

Not even half an hour had passed when a voice, a whispered shout, hailed out of the shadows opposite the cave, '¿Cuando vendrá este tío cabo?' (When will that guy come, corporal?)

'¡Joder! García, ya no vendrá ni el, ni nadie.' A large man stomped out of the cave. 'Venga salir todos, vámonos que el García ya levanto la liebre.' (Bloody hell! Garcia, now neither he nor anyone will come. Come on out, everyone, let's go now that Garcia has sent a message to the hare.)

Suddenly, men came out from behind trees all around, armed with shotguns. They looked like hunters, the type who pursue little rabbits down their holes. Well, needless to say, I fought down my desire to throw stones at them and run around in the dark so that they would shoot each other.

It took a good while till I was completely satisfied that the coast was clear. I took off my clothes and went into the stream to find calm and serenity in nature's bosom. It was fresh, sharp, and so very good. I breathed in the night scents, like the honeysuckle, wild rose, mint, thyme, and so many other plants contributing to this incredible bouquet. An orchestra of nature added to the aura, with its many players each contributing a sound, like the cicadas, owls, night birds, and an occasional nightingale.

And then it all stopped. Silence descended on the woods. There was a presence, something ominous walked the night. A small stone plopped into the water beside me and another hit my ear. I heard a voice.

'And we were worried about you, Moon. And you here, relaxing after an evening's fun.'
I spun my head round, the voice was familiar, it was Ruben.

'We followed the search parties, although Maria knew where you were. I told you she was a strange girl. She was crazy at the start when you disappeared, but you know what it's like with women, she wanted to kill that Toñi. But then she got into a state, crying and saying you were in danger. Anyway, tell you later.'

He pulled off his clothes and came into the stream with me.
'Just lie back and smell it, listen to it,' I said to him.

And so Ruben came back into my life. He asked me what it was, and I answered, 'It's where we came from, and to where we will return.'

Later, we set off on foot to join Mahatma and the others. Ruben told me little more. He seemed quite secretive, although happy to have found me.

'You'll see for yourself, man. No seas pesao, Moon.' (Don't be a nuisance, Moon)

'Don't call me Moon.' I threw a punch at his shoulder,

He jumped around and threw feinted blows into the air, breathing out rapidly and loudly, as boxers do.

'Moony, Moony. Mr moon. Man on the moon, loon.'

It was then that we heard it, a sound. I can't say it sounded like a twig snapping as someone stepped on it, because it didn't. In fact it sounded more like someone swearing. So we waited in a small hidden hollow in the undergrowth. Then we heard more.

'Cabrones, mira que corren.' (Bastards, why are they in such a hurry)

And, with another breath, 'A que los dejo tirao, que se pierdan.' (I bet you I'll leave them on their own, let them get lost)

I jumped out from my hiding spot, and Richa leapt straight up into the air.

'Ave Maria Santísima.'

I hadn't realised before how he said that all the time. I gave him a hug. 'Perdóname, Richa. Es que vinieron a buscarme, y luego llego mi amigo, que los venia siguiendo. Este es Rubén, y este mi casi hermano Richa.' (Forgive me, Richa. It's just that people came searching for me, and then my friend arrived, he was following them. This is Ruben, and this is my near brother, Richa.)

'Sí se nota lo de hermano por el esfuerzo para abrazaros.' (Yes, the brotherhood is obvious when one sees the difficulty you have in hugging each other.)

'Oye niño un respeto que un servidor podría ser tu padre, o mas.' (Hey, boy, some respect. I could be your father or more.)
'Pues me voy, Richa,' (I am going, Richa) I said, reluctant to leave him after his kindness.

'Y yo también. Desde que La Rudi se lio con uno de la obra, me hecho de la casa, del coche, y encima tuve que ir a un cursillo para los malos tratos, voy amargao. El capataz me paga una porquería, trabajando jornada completa. Pues me vengo con vds. como Sancho Panza.' (And I also. Since La Rudi got involved with a labourer, she threw me out of the house, of the car, and to crown it all, I had to go to a course to learn how not to ill treat women. I am a little bitter. The foreman pays me a rubbish wage, working the whole day. So I'm coming with you, like Sancho Panza.)

So Richa came with us, to where, only Ruben knew. My one objection was his allusion to himself as so unfortunate a literary personality as Sancho Panza. One would therefore have assumed that his perception of me would have been as some sort of mad traveller idiot, whose prime form of entertainment was fighting with windmills. Come to think of it, no, I didn't really want to dwell on it.

Casa Pramanas.

The old farmhouses and buildings could be seen from where we stood. They appeared to have been thrown together in a haphazard fashion over the years. Thick creepers had completely covered the walls, giving the house an unreal look in the early morning light. There must once have been an original farmhouse with its adjoining paddock and stables covering about one acre, all enclosed by a high stone wall. As the years progressed, the farmhouse would have grown larger, and progressively new construction started along the wall. Everything was built in the old artisan way, with stone and mortar. The roofs, which once would have been thatched, were now covered in the least costly fashion, with asbestos, corrugated metal, and some red tiling. Over the gate to the paddock hung a large wooden sign. Inscribed upon it boldly, yet with a fine hand, was the motto, Casa Pramanas.

I was later told that the house had been used as a school during the civil war, and there were tales of how a squadron of Franco's Moroccan Regulares had trapped some men from the town there. The walls still told the story of the final massacre.

A yellow and red glow of early sunlight could be seen on the horizon as we arrived. We had been walking all night, dragging Richa along with us. Since the hunters had come and my last contact with my stream and my cave home, some five or six hours had passed. You could see Casa Pramanas silhouetted as the sun was not yet fully risen. We were standing on a hill. A gateway signalled that we were at the boundary to the estate. From the gateposts on each side sprang miles and miles of fencing in both directions, protecting the fields and crops from marauders and keeping the livestock in during winter. Around us, all lay silent and deadly still, with hayfields sweeping to the horizons that were the limits of the valley, and of the estate we had just entered. We walked down the path leading to the farm and the river, and as we approached the paddock gate, dogs began barking and an old country man came out and opened for us.

'Hola,' we said. He grunted and spat.

'Gracias, Geronimo. ¿Cómo te va amigo?' (Thank you, Geronimo. How are you doing, friend?) Ruben continued, unfazed.

'Jodido. ¿Oiga, y este, este viene con vds?' (Very bad, listen. And this one, is this one with you?) We had forgotten Richa, who had just now caught up. So we left him, smoking a ducados and exchanging pleasantries, with the old-timer.

'He moans for everything, it's in his blood. Right now, he's in high spirits. He had a shot of anis del mono in his Manzanilla. He says it starts his flora functioning. He must have gotten something right though, as he's eighty-eight and going like a train.'

'Must be his charm. Could we find something to eat? I'm famished and someone's cooking, can you smell it? Bacon.' I was desperate.

'Let's follow our noses, then.'

We went into one of the various interconnected houses constructed against the side of the paddock wall. Out back, it emerged onto a massive porch with a huge table. Sixty or more people were sitting around it. Jugs and plates were piled high with bread and food, the smells of coffee and cooking wafting invitingly from the laden table and adjacent kitchen. Everyone was speaking in low voices, either contemplating the incredible sunrise over the river and gardens, or because it was still very early and many were still drowsy. As people saw us walk in, the voices became whispers. They gestured silently to Ruben in greeting, and he, mutely and with a smile, returned their hellos. A bit like one would expect the refectory in a monastery to be like, so peaceful at that delicate and wonderful hour of the day. We grabbed the two nearest empty seats, and I took a huge piece of toasted bread and loaded it with everything, all the while smiling around politely. I had been on a diet of wild fruit for long enough and could have eaten a camel. I helped myself to a beverage out of one of the jugs, orange or something, and tucked in. I felt like a dog with his bone, just settled down and defying all and sundry to approach and be threateningly growled at.

And then Ruben, completely out of the blue, dropped his bombshell. He had his mouth completely full when he spoke. 'I didn't tell you, man. Something very strange, uncanny, happened to our Maria.'

I cocked my head to one side, 'The poetry girl?'

'Scars appeared all over her and her arm broke, on its own. Her eyes swelled up like balloons and her nose got broken.'

'How did that happen?' I was aghast.

'No one has any idea, but her mum and this Indian fakir chap, Mr Rafiq, have a theory that it was some sort of mystic connection to you.'

'What are you talking about? I was miles away, you know that?' But it was useless appealing to Ruben and his common sense. 'And how is she now? Can I see her?' My mind was racing, Mystic connection to me? Whatever are they saying?

'Oh, she recovered completely, in a day.' He spluttered, choking on his food. 'Should be here.'

So I stood up and looked around. There were many faces, but then we spotted each other simultaneously, and she waved her hand.

'Hi, Masuhun.' She skipped over and squashed in between us on the bench. 'I'm so happy Ruben found you. I was so worried. I got some sort of feeling you were in trouble, you know, like a telepathic premonition, or like happens with identical twins. I thought you were in very bad danger, but you're OK?'

'Five nights ago, some hooded men beat me up. They nearly killed me.'

She went white when I said it.

'I knew it, Masuhun, I knew it. Did they break your arm?'
'Here,' I showed her. 'But it's all gone now.'

She showed me her arm. It was unscathed.
'They broke mine, also. It's so scary, but I think all they did to you, they did to me as well. And it was also five nights ago. It's so spooky, don't you think? And what else did they do?' she asked me, I imagine, to see if it had happened to her also.

So I told them, I told her and Ruben about it all, about how they hurt me and the mother appearing and what I did, how I grabbed the rock and attacked them. 'And it all happened to you, also. It must have been so frightening! It just happened suddenly. Your mother and brother must have gone nuts. It's crazy, isn't it?' Then it began to dawn on me. 'Or perhaps it's not so crazy,' I blurted out. 'Your name is Maria. Maria, how strong is your faith?'

She looked at me as if I were drunk. 'My faith? Well, I believe in God and in Mary and Jesus. And strong? Well, it's belief; I believe.'

I kissed her then; she was another Richa.

She pushed me away. 'I hardly know you,' she said.

And just for being so coy and demure, I kissed her again, and then said I was sorry and mollified her to stop her from standing up and leaving.
'I also believe,' said Ruben. 'Strongly.' He looked at me, pouting his lips.

Maria smiled. She always smiled at Ruben; she didn't want to, but couldn't help it. So I smiled also, just because she was so nice, and Ruben was an idiot.

'But let me explain,' I insisted. I noticed Mahatma and a striking older woman had discreetly joined us, and together with other people around, were quietly listening in. 'I asked my father what a given name meant. He replied that a name may mean lots more than we ever realise, that perhaps the child is born already bearing that name. Your name is Maria, who knows anything really? Also the ship that rescued me from the sea, from drowning, was the MV Maria. And of course the old lady said, an old lady, who I met at Jimena –'

'Was she a Jewess?'

'Yes,' I answered. 'How did you know?'

It was the striking woman who had asked.

'I am Maria's mother,' she said. 'Because, the Jewess has appeared before, at los Angeles, Jimena.'

'Well, she, the old lady, the Jewess, said that I would be only one of the many upon whom the notion and subsequent conviction will fall in all corners of the world, and will be the new chance for mankind to survive. So maybe Maria is one of the ones upon who the notion has settled.'

'And what may that notion consist of?' This time the speaker was a big Indian with a beard. He was dressed in Indian robes and looked like a Taliban, the ones you see on the TV news.

'I have no idea at all,' I said, shrugging my shoulders. 'Although I do have my suspicions.'

'I think we share suspicions,' Maria looked over at me. 'The notion starts with faith. Is that right, Masuhun?'

I nodded. 'Then we see and we live and we choose, and of course we question, we question ruthlessly. We choose the path of, to use a biblical word, righteousness; we reject evil. And the notion will descend upon us. It will be as a ripple in an ocean made by a rogue asteroid falling from the heavens.'

Someone clapped. I looked up, and saw it was the Taliban and another Indian man and woman.

'It is a good notion. Anyway, we can do nothing. Perhaps the boy Masuhun should continue with his quest, and Maria will be with him, who knows what may happen?'

Looking at me he bowed slightly. 'I am Rafiq. And my wife, Mrs Rafiq, and this is my dear friend, Mr Chagri, who has kindly agreed to cook us an Indian meal for the evening. Thank you.'

Then Mr Chagri stood up, and Ruben muttered loudly, 'Here comes the show.'

Mr Chagri was tall, with a wide moustache and a long angular, and somewhat comical, face.

'I am Chagri. Hello, hello. Ta ta, ta ta. I am Englishman from England. I have my friends in England, Mr Rafiq, Mr Uddin, Mr Choudry, Mr Mushtaq, so I am Englishman, speak English. Today make special Indian food, Cheema Peas, real lamb, good lamb, halal and Indian roti and rice. Before cook for many sheikhs, kings, English lord, Englishman. Today make here food. Thank you, ta ta.'

We ran off, the three of us, into the garden and down to the river.

'Oh yes, please, ta ta, hello hello, oh yes, thank you, I am from Rawalpindi, very close to New Delhi. My name is Patel, Ruben P Patel. Yes, I said Patel with a P, yes P Patel, not b no, no.'

'Shut up, Ruben, for heaven's sakes, and tell us what happened. Tell us your version of the Maria story.'

'Yes do, Ruben, please.'

'For you, missy Maria. Oh yes, please, we were crazy. Her mother wanted to get an ambulance, but Mahatma made her wait a night. We didn't want police and doctors running around accusing everyone. We nursed her. And in the morning, the scars began to disappear. Then the arm righted itself. She had been hysterical before it happened, saying that you were in danger. You see, Moon –'

I let it go, wanting him to continue.
'Five nights ago, Maria had a hysterical attack, screaming your name and asking for help, saying you were in mortal danger, that they would kill you. We took her to her bed, and Mahatma and her mother gave her a mild natural sedative. Suddenly the screaming stopped, and her body started having violent spasms. She started bruising up and wounds opened all over her. Her eyes swelled and one of her arms twisted itself, somehow, and her mother said she could feel a greenstick fracture; the arm was almost irretrievably broken. As you will imagine, we were all gripped by terror for Maria, and Boadicea, that's her mum, actually

called out an ambulance and medics, but Mahatma cancelled it, asking her to wait till morning.

'Well in the morning, late, she began to heal. It was not immediate, but over a twenty-four hour period, everything not only healed, but completely disappeared. And that was when we decided she was malingering.'

We ignored him. The river was inviting and the sun was hot, so we stripped down to decency and jumped in. We looked at each other. Her face was beautiful in a very individual way, she was no more than sixteen or seventeen. Lines were already formed round her mouth, lines made by soft smiles, compassion, being loved and loving.

She gazed dreamily out of her enormous brown almond eyes into mine and stretched out her hand to caress my face.

'"Moreno de verde luna. Anda despacio y garboso, sus empavonados bucles, le brillan entre los ojos."' (Dark skinned with moonlit face. He walks slowly and gracefully, his hanging golden curls shine between his eyes.) She again quoted Lorca.

I felt so fulfilled, and yet we had only just begun to be together. I continued the quote from Lorca. '"A la mitad del camino, corto limones redondos, y los fue tirando al agua, hasta que la puso de oro."' (Halfway along the path, he cut round lemons, and he threw them into the water, until he made it golden.)

And then I took her into my arms and held her very, very tightly. I kissed her, and she kissed me.

Then the Richa suddenly appeared.

'There's your mate, the cave dweller, come to gawk at your new bird. I'll take him with me to the kitchen to see how the fakir's friend is planning to poison us all tonight.'

His English was too good, he used phrases I had never heard. 'He speaks good English. Actually, so do you.'

'We should, his parents are both English, and so's my mother.'

'Is she true to her name? You know, Boadicea.'

'Yes, she is but not in a Spanish liberated woman type of way. My mother loved my father till he died and was always a faithful, very feminine wife. But she is strong, believe me, she has a will like a rod of steel.'

'Why doesn't she take a new man? Doesn't she find it lonely?'

'Well there's more than one answer to that story. She loved my father, he was a musician and died of cancer ten years ago. It's a bit like the Clara Schumann story. Did you know that Robert Schumann, as a boy, used to go to piano lessons at Clara's father's house. He would dress up as a ghost to scare Clara. They became close, and had to fight her father in open court to be able to marry. When Robert died as a result of his recurring mental disease, Brahms, a close friend of the family, proposed marriage to Clara, mainly so as to be able to care for her and her four children. She refused, saying that she wanted to dedicate the rest of her life to the memory of Robert. She did this by giving concerts of his music all over Europe. She was of course an accomplished concert pianist.

'If love comes along, my mother'll be swept off her feet like a tender girl. She's one of those people, men and women, who are romantics and would never have sex for its own sake, as is done all the time in this country by so many people. I believe it also happens throughout Europe and the West. They don't seem to realise that the best of what they had has been taken from them, and replaced with a tawdry consumer product. Boadicea's life is so full anyway, and love will probably find her when the time comes. It makes me angry, however, to see what they've turned human affection and sexuality into. People should only ever join together for love, the way it's meant, and that love should bear fruit, the fruit of love.'

'What about lust or desire? How should people control their lust?'

'Everything in today's society is designed to stimulate lust— pictures, porn, ads, everything. Add to that the aphrodisiac effects of alcohol and you create a roaring sex beast. Ideally, we should control our appetites with will power and prayer, it's not really such a big deal in a normal world. Anyway, there are so many other things, culture, music, literature, interests. But right now, it's bedtime for you. You look dead on your feet.'

I was exhausted, having walked all night. I was taken to a dormitory by Maria. She pulled back the sheets and I brushed her face with a kiss, 'Después hablamos.' (We'll talk later) I immediately dropped into a deep sleep.

I dreamt of the sea, and rocks and waves. We were disembarking, and everyone helped each other. I slipped on a wet rock, and strong hands were there to heave me up. I helped a man who fell at my side, a black man. He muttered, 'Thank you, my braada.'

I looked into his face as he smiled, but it was not William, not the shak.

Looking back, I could see helmeted soldiers, fighters robed in white tunics. They were on the boats and the shore, holding back hordes of evil looking serpents. We climbed some steep rocky steps, it was raining and the steps were slippery, I kept falling and slipping, but no one held you back they helped each other, some would push me ahead, and I would do the same for the weaker ones I found in my path.

I awoke, showered, and set off through the house in search of Ruben and Maria. They were drinking tea on the big porch, having also just awakened. The creepers we had seen covering the house were releasing their fragrance into the air, and the scents of jasmine, stephanyotis, honeysuckle, and all sorts of sweet smelling plants perfumed the evening air so that it was an adventure trying to decide which scent was which. The mosquitos and flies were noticeably absent, repelled by the same plants that gave off such delightful perfumes. During the day, the house helpers hung small plastic bags filled with water from every rafter and at every vantage point to the porches and the house. The theory was that a fly, seeing its image magnified in the bag, would get scared and run, and amazingly, it worked.

'Why did you go off with her?' she asked.

Her attitude towards me had changed in just a few hours. Not knowing who, or what, had got into her mind, I didn't answer her, not wanting to play a game.

'Look, Maria, I know you and Toñi hardly at all. It seems now that Toñi is a bad person, or at least surrounded by things which are potentially evil. And you, well, now is when we can get to know each other. It seems as if in any case we have been thrown together by forces outside of our understanding.'

'So a hasty marriage is definitely out of the question? It'll just need to be slowly falling in love?'

'Shut up, Ruben,' she said sideways, not even glancing at him.

'And you need to be very careful, Moon. In Europe and the West, the powers that be are busy creating the new woman. The new woman looks for sex, laughs at love, and only ever marries to have children, and, of course, to have someone around to change the nappies and push the pram.'

'You're just miffed, cause you can't find a girl,' she jeered.

'They do scare me, actually,' Ruben mused. 'But nowadays, I can always be gay.'

'Gay is something you're born with,' I quickly interjected. 'It should never be something you choose because you're lonely or can't get a girl.'

'So what's your plan then, Moon?'

'Well, for starters, we can be serious. Think of all the bad stuff going down all over the planet just so that you guys can sit in the West and be flippant. And it's not Moon, Ruby.'

'He's not being flippant. He just is like that. I'll admit I'm really afraid of what happened to me, but tell me, what happened at Toñi's house? I really do deserve to know.'

'Not that again? Heavens, Toñi wanted to be intimate, and for me to be like them, phones and computers and sex and drugs and alcohol, so I just left. Then I got beaten up, and the lady appeared in my head and I defended myself. And now I'm accused of murder, which is a lie. So I have to go follow my…whatever. Go to where my father sent me. You see, even to not have an activity, to just stay still, is wrong for me.'

'Well,' she said, 'believe it or not, us, we, here in this humble place in a corner of the country, are also fighting our own little battle for order and sanity in this mad world.'

Ruben and Maria both attended a local school. Most of their free time revolved around Casa Pramanas. Friends would come to Casa Pramanas to swim, hang out, or share homework. Ruben still lived with his parents, who also lived at Pramanas. Maria explained, 'We have paying and non-paying guests. Everyone works in the fields, and there are always things happening. You can check out the notice board later. Today, for example, we're still in time, we can go and participate in the martial arts gathering. Everyone goes and either stretches or does everything, you can get as involved as you wish. The maestro is a really qualified guy in various martial arts and talks nonstop throughout the session, but he's hilarious.'

Boadicea had returned home from the east years ago and married a musician. Her grandfather had left her a small building which was one of the cluster that was Casa Pramanas. She was one of the first teachers of yoga in the country, and then thought of renting out rooms to visitors. The surrounding houses in the cluster were in a ruinous state. Guests who could ill afford to pay would pay her in labour. Slowly, they improved the properties, which she bought for a song over the years. A man from the mountain town of Ronda who was staying as a working guest said to her that he would make a garden in the plot of land she owned in front of the house. The garden worked out and provided food for the entire household. So she slowly bought more and more land, again for next to nothing, until she owned the whole valley, about thirty hectares. The man from Ronda ran everything, and later, when Mahatma returned from his travels, he joined them. There was a live in lady administrator and a house manageress.

The attractions to paying and also to working guests were many, to live and work in nature, eat ecologically, totally and consistently. They were able to tap into experts on yoga, Vedic astrology, Ayurvedic plant life and healing, martial arts and well-being. Wi-Fi and telephone coverage was only available for two hours per day, and never on weekends. Only people working in the computer department, or professionals living as paying guests at the Casa had six hours per day access, and no weekends. Guests and friends of the Casa were strongly discouraged from connecting to the internet or its so-called social networks.

An Indian gentleman named Mr Rafiq was a retired professor of Vedic astrology and had meetings, he disliked calling them lessons. He was once a professor of the subject at an Indian university, so was terribly well qualified.

Mrs Rafiq, his wife, who was steeped in Ayurvedic plant culture, was busy importing seeds from all over to cultivate plants and make them available at a small price to growers and enthusiasts everywhere. Mrs Rafiq was very angry with all those large companies who were genetically sterilising plants strains all over the world. Genetic criminals, she called them.

'I am busy always holding down the fort for the seeds of the planet,' she said to me when I was introduced to her. 'One day, new legislation will be introduced to curb this terrible activity conducted by major companies in the name of their own profit and monopoly. Can you imagine an earth, our home planet, where the only seeds you can find are by purchasing them off these people, and that these seeds will grow and blossom once only and never again. This, because they have been sterilised, castrated, genetically modified by these criminals. There are at least twenty-five thousand plants usable in Ayurvedic medicine to be saved, so please excuse me, I must get on.' She turned to leave, but then turned back to me with a parting shot, 'One more thought, Mr Moon.'

It's that Ruben again, just wait till I get him.

'Think, Mr Moon, if these rascals do this today to plants, who's to stop them doing it tomorrow to human beings? After all, mass obligatory sterilisation is nothing new to humanity, and it certainly did not start or end with the Nazis. People, human beings, were forcibly sterilised in America and European countries shortly before the world wars.'

It seemed as if Boadicea had heard us talking about her. She suddenly materialised out of the kitchen.

'Masuhun, you will forgive me, but I need some more answers, would you mind?'

She sat down with the three of us, carrying a jug and four glasses. The jug was filled with lots of ice and a lemon coloured liquid.

'Is that what I think it is?' I asked.

'It's manna, manna from heaven.'

I smiled at her and held out my glass. She filled it, the ice plopping and splashing as it fell, and I drank it down with relish—crushed, sun-dried limes from Abu Dhabi.

'How did you recover so quickly, Masuhun?'

'It was an old lady, she washed me and gave me a sleeping draught. It was in a dream. She applied salves to my wounds and creams to my body, gave me water from a sponge, and washed all of me, even my most intimate parts, which were in pain. Then she gave me a sleeping draught, and, I imagine, set my arm.'

'So an old lady in a dream completely healed your broken body in a day, and also that of my daughter, by transference? It was you who actually suffered a beating, and for some reason, the resultant bodily condition was physically conveyed to my daughter. She suffered all your ills and your subsequent recovery.' She said it loudly. 'Stigmata! As Francis of Assisi or St Thomas suffered the wounds of Christ. I have had lots of experience with these things in my travels.'
She looked me straight in the face. 'Never have I seen anything like this. This was for real, terribly real. I have witnessed and seen the results of happenings with Yajurvedi in India, Macumba or Umbanda in Brazil, or shamanism in many parts of the world, and in most cases, they lacked authenticity. But this, never did I see the like. We only see and believe that this was an incredible manifestation of Good, of the agents of Good righting evils.'

Mahatma joined in with his customary growl. 'I told them your story as you told me, and frankly, we found it a bit weak.'

'A bit weak?' I jumped to my feet. 'A bit weak? What do you mean, a bit weak? It's all the truth, all there is,' I shouted.

'We believe you, Masuhun. What I'm trying to say is that all this is happening because of you and your quest. There must be something about you that we don't know, that not even you know.'

'No, I think we understand, I do and Maria does. It's you, you have to come to grips with yourself and decide that you believe. We are younger, fresher, perhaps more innocent, and disappointed with the way humans are destroying the world. And as Maria said before, once the notion begins to descend on people all over the planet, hundreds, millions of people, it will be as a ripple in an ocean made by a rogue asteroid falling.'

'And as you told us earlier, all this was told to you at los Angeles, Jimena de la Frontera, by an old lady who appeared to you, and she told you she was a Jewess?'

I nodded.

'La judía, la monja judía, es una leyenda. Murió hace cientos de años dicen que es enviada de la Señora, de la virgen. A este niño hay que guardarlo y ayudarlo en su camino. Algo sobrenatural se nos esta manifestando, y habiendo visto y oído al chaval creo que el es un vehículo inocente de la bondad. Y, que el Señor nos proteja, porque parece que mi Maria, mi niña algo tiene que ver también con todo esto es como una protectora de el.' (The Jewess, the Jewish nun is a legend. She died hundreds of years ago, and the legend is that she is a messenger sent by the Virgin. This boy must be protected and helped on his road. Something supernatural is manifesting itself to us, and having heard and seen the boy, I believe that he is a naïve vehicle for good. And may the Good Lord protect us, because it seems that my Maria, my girl, has some connection with all this, as if it were her destiny to protect him.)

Suddenly, the professor, Rafiq, strode in and bowed to us all.

'Masuhun, you told us your father sent you to search for a mother and child, a Roman Catholic virgin, an effigy, a statue. Is that correct?'

'Yes, sir, it is. Why do you ask?'

'Can you recall his exact words? I know this may be rather upsetting for you.'

I gestured gently indicating that it was not a problem, and then I cast my mind back to that terrible day. I could see my father, Afra, shrunken and still, and I longed to hold him and keep him safe.

'He spoke these words,' I said, my voice faltering. 'He said, "Masuhun, go and find the stone on which the mother appears. Ask her for help for you and your people. She will listen to you, you are named for her son."'

Mr Rafiq started to get agitated. 'You see, you see it's not the mother you seek. Well, it is, but you will only find her at the stone on which the mother appears. Well the mother in Jimena, los Angeles, now known as La Señora de los Angeles, as well as the mother here in Medina Sidonia and in many places in this region, are all replicas of the same effigy. The original, or its place of origin, is what you are seeking. The virgin in los Angeles is the one brought in holy procession in the fourteenth century. Am I right, Masuhun? On the right track?'

'Yes, very right. Please continue.'
'In 1309, Ferdinand the fourth of Castile, whose armies were laying siege to Algeciras, found that supplies were getting to the besieged city through Gibraltar. The Duke of Guzman, acting for King Ferdinand, took the rock. Later, Ferdinand, grateful for his victories, ordered the founding of a sacred shrine to the mother at the southernmost point of Gibraltar. A chapel was built on the ruins of an existing mosque. Ferdinand named the lady the virgin of all Europe, Our Lady Of Europa. The Arabs retook the rock in 1333, and the Virgin was taken by her faithful to a place of safety behind Christian lines. We understand that she was taken to Jimena de la Frontera, a convent, which today is the sanctuary of La Señora de los Angeles. So, the stone on which the mother appears, in Masuhun's father's words, is the place where this procession came from.'

'But how can I go there?' Suddenly, I was excited. I knew where I needed to go. To Gibraltar, the Shrine of the Lady Of Europa.

'Tomorrow, we will plan.' Mahatma stood up. 'Tonight, the dining room is needed, as the Indian food smells quite delicious.'

Thine enemy.

I guess, looking back on it now, in spite of believing, my mind had not really given total credit to all the rigmarole that had been building up around my father's deathbed request. But people, it seemed to me, were just desperate to believe in something that was pure and not a lie. This brave new world I was discovering, with all its incredible new discoveries and progress, had along the way shed much of the simple values that people in less advanced societies still held sacred.

We slept that night in our bunks, in the dormitory for single guys that Maria had taken me to earlier. I made Ruben take the lower bunk because his talk of ring of fire had me worried.

'It wasn't that hot.'

'Just you wait, Moon. We're not accustomed to it. These Indian guys eat chili sandwiches for breakfast.'

'I'm leaving tomorrow, Ruben, on my own.'

He went silent, but after a long while he stated, 'I'm coming with you, Moon. Or are you thinking of taking Richa?'

We both laughed at the thought.

In the morning, the plan was to go out to the fields with the rest. We would then escape back to the house before arriving at our allotted place of work. All went according to plan, but as we re-entered the dining area, Ruben said, 'Oh, oh.'

I saw we were being beckoned by a man sitting at a table. The room was pleasantly silent, a change from the usual hum of activity. A man and a woman were sitting in a very relaxed fashion, reading. He had a copy of the English Times held up for his scrutiny, and she something called Punch.

'Hello, darling. Do be a sweetie and get two extra cups from the kitchen,' she said, not looking up. 'There's plenty of tea in the pot. Still warm, I'd say.'

'Fellow in the kitchen gave it to me, piping. Nice chap. Paki, I think.' He glanced at her ever so briefly, then noticed us again. 'Well, Ruben, do the honours.'

'Papa, Mammy, this is Masuhun, alias Moon, although the Moon hasn't quite been accepted by polite society yet. Moon, this is my mammy, Bernadette, and my pater, Horatio.'

She smiled graciously at me, and I felt as if I should bow. She had a graceful nonchalance that made me feel as if I was in the presence of royalty. Horatio pushed his Times to one side, removed his spectacles, and extended a strong hand, which I shook. He looked nothing like Ruben. Ruben was small, dark, and thin, attractive in a dishevelled sort of fashion, dark hair all over the place. This man was long legged and large all over, with blondish hair pushed back, and wearing steel-rimmed glasses.

'Hello, old boy. Had a rough run, I hear. Still, it's all character building. No harm done by the looks of it.' He spoke very plum in mouth, the badge of the British upper classes. I was told once that it was beaten into them at public school.

He then went back to his paper whilst Bernadette poured the tea. I now understood what the British meant by stiff upper lip.

'Drop of milk, goes first you know, cold. After all, we did invent tea, you know. He does like his nicknames, called me Bins years ago, and it stuck. I did rather like Bernadette. The British always were terrible name callers. I mean that poor man in the kitchen is a Paki. And then you've got wogs, wops, Eyties, Aussies. Oh, and their ladies are Sheilas, although I think they themselves call them that.'

'We're Guiris here in Spain, mammy. And here's a good one, in Cuba, if you're an old boy or old girl, visitor of course, searching after young meat, you become a tembo or temba wanikiki.'

'You won't find Muslims thinking up names for people; far too respectful. All of these Koranic cultures are like that. Look at that Chagri and Rafiq, gentlemen in every way,' Horatio put in as his contribution.

'They're Hindus, papa.'

'Then they'd be named Ravi or Rajit. I certainly won't let you near my crossword. Hindus! Do something with the boy, Bins.'

After tea, we left Horatio with his crossword and Bins with her Punch. We went into the kitchen, where Mr Chagri had prepared a bag of food and drink for each of us to take.

'Hush hush,' Ruben said to him, holding a finger to his lips.

'Oh, yes, please sah. Hush hush hush.'

Casa Pramanas is accessible either by fording the river, which, given its width and current state, was not a popular choice, or, some three miles upriver, there is a bridge that is well maintained as it also serves to carry a massive freshwater aqueduct for the surrounding area. A third option is to head out over the hills, through fields and valleys, that's the route Ruben brought me along at the start.

We chose to cross with the aqueduct bridge. Instead of taking the most obvious and speediest route to the bridge by following the river and the track that wound along beside it, we decided for the sake of prudence to cut inland.

After walking away from the river for some half a mile, we turned right. Ruben was adamant that no one lived in the quadrant between us and the river and that there were no dwellings. Yet we could hear dogs barking, as well as see and smell wood smoke.

We decided to climb the only rise around in order to see what was happening. Ruben had brought some field glasses so we would be able to identify what was going on, if anything at all. Our route was quite heavy going, although from below it had looked easy. We arrived at the summit panting and gasping, and lay down at the edge looking out over the river.

Through the glasses, we could make out several men standing by the bridge, and about two hundred yards away from the river in our direction, there were quite a few men, a campfire, and two vans. We saw a car arrive at the bridge and stop at the apparent behest of the men there. The car was checked, the boot opened, and then they were waved on.

Then we looked towards the main road, and on the roundabout that distributed traffic to the various towns in the area was a Guardia Civil checkpoint. My heart fell, it must have been me they were after, the Guardia wanted me for murder. I put that mentally to one side, as otherwise, the whole idea of going on weighed too heavily upon me.

'So this lot can't be Guardia, in fact they aren't police, either,' I mused to Ruben. 'I think we've got a long trek ahead of us, we really will need to go the long route.'

'The question is, Moon, shall we enjoy our picnic now, or later?'

I couldn't believe it, the guy was incorrigible. So I just set off back down the rise with Ruben in my wake, heading towards the long route. We hadn't gone that far when two men suddenly materialised out of the undergrowth before us. They were big and dressed in combat fatigues. I shouted out to Ruben and tried running back up the hill, and when I saw they were following turned to face them. Then the leading one was upon me, so I sidestepped and blocked, but was swept aside by a glancing blow from his foot which I had not seen coming. I looked up from where I had fallen. I was unhurt but waiting for another blow to fall. This time I was not alone however, my assailant was suddenly engrossed in trying to deal with a flurry of kicks to the head being delivered by a Ruben I had not seen before. The guy just folded as Ruben delivered his coup de grace. And metres away, the other man was being pulled apart by a large ninja.

'You all right, Moon¬¬?' Ruben called breathlessly.

'Sure, thanks. But what's happening, who's that guy?' It was obvious he was protecting us, but who was he, for heaven's sake?

'Oh, of course! Heavens, well, have a guess. Who's the ninja? No, it's not Mahatma, no it's not Richa, it's gracious Horatio, Papa, of course.'

The ninja started up towards us, pulling off his balaclava. Indeed, it was Ruben's father. I never would have believed it! I had him down as an intellectual, totally non-physical person. I started to feel bad, as I really had misjudged them, all of them, probably, That's why I wanted to go alone. I thought they lived in this milk and honey country, in a pampered existence, much of it at the expense of the rest of the world that was out there suffering. But now I realised that what I had seen as indifference was really a cover for these profoundly caring people's concern for others.

'Sorry, chaps, had to get involved. Saw them playing games around here at least twenty-four hours ago. No idea who they are. Probably eastern Europeans, mercenaries of some sort. They spotted you boys on the ridge. I'd hazard there are some more on their way, so let's get back to the casa, advise the Guardia.' I had a sudden vision of him tranquilly donning his ninja garb as he continued eyeing his Times crossword, then striding purposefully out of the casa, after having carefully put the caddy on the pot, saying, 'Keep it piping.'

We tied up the men using rope Horatio had slung around his waist, and left them for the Guardia, whom we phoned from the house, after returning sheepishly, tails between our legs. Horatio had removed his ninja clothing as we went, and hid it in a plastic bag.

'No advertising, old boy. Keep it quiet. Don't worry, only Mahatma and I know you went, so no one else is even remotely aware that you absconded. Apart from your batman, Moon, you'd better sort him out. Tell him that, mum's the word.'

I looked at Ruben who, with a deadpan expression, explained what Horatio had meant, especially the bit about batman.

'Richa is your batman, and apparently he controls you from afar.'

Horatio phoned the authorities to report the two men as having tried to assault him and his son when they were out for a walk, and that there was an encampment of them by the bridge. 'Probably eastern Europeans burglarizing homes in the area, armed.'

Unfortunately, we didn't get to see the resulting Guardia raid. It would have been very Hawaii Five-0, with lots of sirens and drama; they did enjoy that sort of stuff here, unless any shooting started up that would have set the cat amongst the pigeons.

'Well, I still need to go,' I said loudly before losing their attention to the Times and an Indian picnic.

Horatio looked up at the clock, 'It's zero nine thirty hours now. Mahatma's study at eleven hundred for a briefing, chaps. And now, if you'll excuse me.'

We left him heading, teapot in hand, to the kitchen for some piping hot tea, I imagine. Bins had disappeared, probably busy pruning roses in the garden. Ruben dragged me to a quiet secluded table at the far end of the porch, where he sat down to eat his Indian food, so I followed suit.

We were busily tucking in when we heard, 'Oh yes, please, thank you. Food is good, want tea? Indian tea?'

'Oh, God,' muttered Ruben. 'No, thank you, Mr Chagri.'
'Your mother, Mrs Bins, and your father, Mr John, very nice people. This house feel like Punjab when they live here. They are very British. I too am very English.'

The briefing was at eleven o'clock sharp. Mahatma, Horatio, Maria, Boadicea, Mr Rafiq, and a few unknown men and women were all there.

Ruben looked around, then asked, 'Will we wait for Richa and Mr Chagri?'

Silence reigned. Ruben's reputation preceded him apparently.

Then Mahatma spoke. 'The mission is to get Moon, here, to Europa Point. Tomorrow is the fifth of May, the day of our Lady of Europa. At approximately eighteen hundred hours, a small flotilla of local boats may leave Gibraltar port carrying the effigy of the virgin and transport her by sea to Europa Point. This is unconfirmed, though. I only mention it, as it may serve as a blind. Ecclesiastics, however, don't seem to know whether they're coming or going.'

'We however, will get Moon to the shrine by nineteen hundred hours, which we understand is when some sort of mass takes place in honour of the mother. Sundown will be at twenty-one twelve, and astro twilight will fall at twenty-two forty-nine. Europa Point is a historical, fortified bastion. Some maps and plans should be here at any time and will be handed around. We shall continue our assessment re the actual arrival once we have those.

'The first phase leaving Casa Pramanas, will be carried out using all of our seventeen vehicles. Second phase will be crossing from La Linea and various points along the Cadiz coast to our target. To receive specific orders—sorry, instructions, thank you—Boadicea and Maria have scheduled appointments for everyone to meet with me and Horatio. Please be prompt.'

'A question, please.' The speaker was a tall, shy looking, heavily moustachioed man at the back. 'Surely, we could pull a few strings and avoid all this?'

Horatio stepped in, 'You're right, of course, or would be if we were aware of who or what we're up against. The boy is on some sort of mystic quest. Sounds far-fetched to us grizzled types, but stranger things have happened. Some of you here know me well, and I'm telling you that what we used to pray about, talk about, and dream of when we had had a gutful of what went on may be about to happen. And this may be our chance to be a part of it. What we do not know is who the enemy is, and it may well be that there are some of ours who have been compromised. Neither do we know, if this were the case, how far up the ranks. So if we just get the boy to the shrine, it will be mission accomplished. We will of course stick around subsequently to see what goes down and if we can help.'

Our briefing was attended by Mahatma, Horatio, Maria, Ruben, Boadicea, one of the unknown men from the meeting earlier, and myself, promptly at sixteen hundred hours, and we were allocated thirty minutes. Mahatma stood at the front and outlined the procedure.

'Information will be given on a need to know basis, for time economy and because it's more expedient. Car number two is Horatio's

Mercedes 600 Saloon, which will carry passengers Moon, Maria, and Ruben. The space between the front and back seats is ample for you guys to ride on the floor until we are well away from Pramanas. The vehicle is old and beaten up, but souped up for performance. We will be in constant radio contact with four other vehicles that will travel with us, separately but together. Be ready to react instantaneously to orders from Horatio re changing cars and so on. The driver is Horatio and his co-driver is Eustace, who will also carry signalling equipment.

'Boadicea, you will lead team one with the BMW 530, again oldish. Keep at least ten miles ahead and advise Mahatma as to hazards. Car three will be driven by Matt, and will house Mahatma as controller. Cars four and five will act as needed under Mahatma's coordination, as will all cars.

'Our destination is one of a selection of beaches and harbours situated all along the La Linea and Algeciras coastal stretches. The coordination work on these, our departure points, as well as the points of landing at Gibraltar, will be established before we depart tomorrow. Zero hour is sixteen hundred hours in the dining area. Be there, please, and be ready.'

'What if all these people work so hard and take risks to get me to the stone, and nothing happens?' I said to Ruben and Maria after the meeting.

'Have faith, Moon, have faith,' they chorused.

'Who's our co-driver, do you know him?'

'Yeah, he's a real moaner, always grumbling about something. You'll see tomorrow. But papa says he's top in his field. That's probably why they haven't shot him yet.'

Deadline Getares.

It was one of those days when, early on, it had seemed as if it would rain. Then, as the morning progressed, it blossomed and turned into a wondrous May day. Yet the threat of rain was always there; after all, April had only just gone. The sky was painted a stunning bright blue, birds were singing everywhere, and the fragrant scents of the creepers hung lightly in the air of the porch, as if it were evening time. Even the plants were confused by the changing of the seasons.

'Lousy weather for it. We'll be seen a mile off. I knew it, I knew it.'

'If it were cloudy Eustace, visibility would be zilch,' replied Ruben. 'And even you like to see the enemy before he sees you and steps on your head, or your fingers.'

'Don't start getting lippy, boy, or you'll get it.'

'Couldn't catch a fly.'

'Leave him alone, Rube, he's our co-driver.'

'Yeah, watch it Rube, or you'll walk.'

It was just minutes to sixteen hundred; our deadline for the beach was eighteen hundred, and the shrine nineteen hundred. I couldn't really see where all the slack time was going. I had checked on the map and we, that is Casa Pramanas, were no more than 80 km, or an hour, away from the beach Horatio had mentioned, Getares.

Cars started leaving with the sound of tyres crunching against hundreds of small gravel pebbles. Some of them had had their number plates changed, and Richa told me they'd also had the number rubbed off the frame. Mahatma was already in place in his control car, complete with earphones and state of the art transmitter receiver, probably disguised, built into the car. Much of this intelligence came from Ruben, who may well have been spinning us a yarn as we sauntered around earlier with Maria and Richa in tow. Horatio and Eustace called us for departure of our own convoy. Ruben started up a running commentary of what he thought was happening,

'Right, our chaps are bursting the first road blocks and running, dumping and changing rides, getting the opposition into a right turmoil. That's all happening on or around the A31 route, the obvious place the hare would run from. There are two possible main routes, the bridge route, which leads onto the A31, and is some 80 km as the crow drives, to our destination; and of course we are going out the back door, with a scout car running up ahead and at least four or five further backup vehicles. Our route will take us to the main Cadiz road, but filters out left to Conil de la Frontera and the main coast highway.'

Boadicea sailed off at a brisk pace to get 10 km ahead of us. Behind, we were trailing a further five cars or so, I estimated. It was all just happening as we went, and very fast. Then Boadicea's voice came over the radio confirming all clear. She apparently had cleared the dirt track and had hit the A road leading towards Cadiz. It was a bit like what you hear in a taxi. All cars calling in to Mahatma, central control. We could hear what sounded like absolute pandemonium from what I supposed were the running cars on the other route, but Horatio had ears only for Boadicea and our own backup vehicles. Boadicea was on again, advising change of direction to the Conil de la Frontera road. It all seemed quiet and running without a hitch on our route, all the Guardia and other searchers must have been pulled off to the A31. Boadicea's voice suddenly changed—something was happening.

'Up ahead! Up ahead! Off the road, at least ten fifteen cars. Playing cat and mouse. OK, I've passed them, they're chasing me. Go the Cadiz route, I'll let them take me, search. I will call once clear.' Then her voice disappeared.

'Will she be OK?' Asked Maria in a small voice.

'Don't worry, it's Moon they want. They'll search the car and let her continue. They'll be searching all the cars that pass till the Guardia catch on.'

'Very reassuring,' I said.

Horatio just laughed.

'What they want and what they get, don't worry boy, they won't get near you.'

So we drove on and hit a motorway system heading towards Cadiz. After a while, we veered left for the Algeciras highway.

Then Boadicea came on again, 'All clear now. Started searching me, then another car appeared so they waved me on. Probably thought I was too sweet and feminine to be involved with you lot. Will continue forward and join you just after where the Conil slip road hits the highway.'

Then it happened—suddenly spread across the road were green uniforms, vans, and cars. Blocking all three lanes were Guardia Civil vehicles, blue lights flashing. Guardsmen were dragging chains across the lanes, to lame runaway cars. Luckily, they had not yet covered lane three, which was where Horatio aimed with an amazing spurt of speed and screeching of tyres. I thought the car would tip over with such a radical direction change at a very high speed. Guardsmen were jumping out of the path of the runaway like clowns at the circus from a stampeding elephant. We were through and running like crazy.

'Bo emergency! Pick the kids up at exit number 26 to Conil, bottom of slip lane, hoot once on arrival. This car will run, sorely compromised, have burst the coop. Bo, confirm understood. Mahatma, confirm received.'

'Understood. Will collect kids and mother hen approximately fifteen minutes. Good luck.'

'Mahatma here. Understood, Horatio. Boadicea, you will be emerging onto highway at exit 34, don't do it, do not go onto highway, proceed forward onto roundabout. Junction letting southbound traffic onto that same roundabout is 26, pickup spot for kids, hoot once, over.'

To hear them, we may well have been back at home drinking tea, rather than in a wild car chase being pursued by half of Spain's paramilitary police force. They were so calm, whilst my mouth was bone dry and I felt a bit nauseous. Ruben was quiet and Maria was shaking like a leaf.

'Mahatma, instruct cars five and six to hang around Conil area, look out for me. OK, kids ready to jump as I slow down, slide into storm ditch, and roll to the bottom, then stay still minimum five minutes. Eustace, stay with them.'

Mother hen, you know who that is?'

'My mistake.' Ruben wasn't quiet, he was just thinking.

He reduced speed from the 250 plus km we must have been travelling at to less than 100. Then he came off the highway, and as he reached the bottom of the slip road, we opened the doors and jumped, then slid down into the mud at the bottom of the storm culvert. We lay there for a good five minutes, with Eustace muttering, 'F-ing kids,' as Ruben giggled.

They certainly didn't allow circumstances to faze them. Maria glanced at me and smiled, shrugging her shoulders. And all this with Guardia Civil vehicles, sirens flashing, racing past on the highway and others down the slip road and towards Conil, where in my mind's eye, I could see them racing after Horatio through the whitewashed lanes and cobbled streets.

The four of us lay in the ditch for what seemed like ages, till a long distinct hoot of a car horn had Eustace moving with unlikely agility to poke his head out of the culvert. We helped Maria onto the road and scrambled out. Luckily, no Guardia cars passed at that exact minute, so we were able to get off OK. Cars five and six announced their arrival at the slip junction number 26 to Conil, eyes peeled for Horatio. We saw them sweep by in a flash as we looked back. It was comforting to know we weren't alone.

So Ruben continued his running commentary.

'Uncompromised vehicles making their way as per brief to allocated marine departure points the length and breadth of Cadiz coast. Readied sea transportation units will be fired up and ready to roll. Time now,' he checked his watch, 'seventeen o-nine. ETA Getares beach, seventeen thirty-eight or so.'

We drove on at a sensible pace down the central lane, so as not to attract attention. Two other cars were behind us, ready to create diversions to attract Guardia attention in case of problems.

'Horatio here. All clear now. I am with car number six rolling towards target. Stay off actual beach on arrival unless under pressure. Wait for me. Procedure will be snatch off sand by fast inflatables.'

'Mahatma here. Our units all clear. Converging on designated marine departure points. Over.'

I breathed a sigh of relief. It seemed that the blockade had been successfully overcome, and we were close to our goal. As we turned off the highway, a car came swinging out of a side road and straight at us. With amazing dexterity, Boadicea set our car onto a course parallel with that of our would-be assailant, and with a burst of speed, shot off ahead with the other car in hot pursuit. Looking back, I saw one of our two remaining backup cars mount the pavement and smash the alien against a projecting façade.

'Mahatma, order immediate snatch off beach. Cannot await Horatio. Moon and friends under imminent threat.'

Then to us, 'Kids, when we stop, beach or pavement, run straight to the water's edge, and don't look back. I don't need to tell you the drill, sergeant,' she addressed Eustace, who was busy setting up what I thought was a small submachine gun that he had pulled out of his bag.

Boadicea set the car right by the small seawall, and we opened the doors and ran. Small arms fire started crackling loudly behind us, and we were alone. Boadicea and Eustace were not with us. We ran and our feet sank in the damp sand. We had scarcely reached the shore, when two very long black rubber Zodiac boats tore up, making a wave of water on the shallows, and two groups of armed men wearing balaclavas, who had been riding on the floats of the boats, came rushing at us. Some grabbed us unceremoniously, and packed us onto one of the craft. The others ran up the beach, and for a minute, the crackle which was gunfire increased, and then stopped altogether. Then Boadicea, Eustace, and Horatio were with us, and the men dragged the boats away from the shore. The pilot gave it throttle, the nose of the inflatables lifted, and suddenly we were at sea.

'Eighteen o-two, gentlemen, ladies. We narrowly missed our eighteen hundred deadline,' said Ruben, looking at his watch. 'Not good enough.'

Everyone laughed. 'Welcome aboard, Major.'

I didn't know what to think, it was becoming apparent that somewhere along the way some army or other had adopted and was helping me. I looked at Ruben and Maria. She was quite pale, so I put an arm around her and gave her a hug.

'Listen up, please! For those of you who don't know me, I am Major Horatio Bullock. We have a further deadline, as we are all aware, and that is to set this young man, Moon, on the actual shrine of our lady of Europa. This together with his friends and ourselves, in case they need protection. It's a short run over the bay, perhaps twenty minutes, but we are anticipating the worst. Right at this moment, friendly boats, larger and smaller, fishing boats and leisure craft manned by friends to act as a sort of phalanx or spearhead, are heading towards us. So pickup is end of Getares beach, Palmones, and Algeciras nautical club. All in all some twelve boats. Oh, and of course we've a couple of craft sailing round from la Atunara on the Med side. Europa Point is a fortified bastion, so we go up the only steps, or scale the walls with ladders, or go round the trinity lighthouse end, or take them to Rosia Bay, where we have fast motorbikes lined up and waiting. In any event, you all have designated access points and tasks which should be carried through in spite of changes in anything else. As was agreed, if the children must scale the walls, they will be carried. A team of three SB chaps and two SR per child, one to carry and his backup; one at the bottom and two at the top of the ladder. If we are challenged by our military, we will acknowledge and identify, no use starting a civil war.'

And so we set off in the centre of a group of craft, which Mahatma and Horatio identified as ours, although there were quite a few other boats milling around in the bay. We were not sure where they were coming from, although looking out to sea, I could see a forest of smaller and bigger craft all over the horizon. They stretched from Algeria to the furthest visible end of the Atlantic. Ruben said that it must have been some sort of optical illusion. He said that's where the Guardia Civil cutter shot off to.

'Probably think it's the year 711 again, and the caliphs are back.'

As we started to travel slowly across the bay, a group of big fast launches waved us back, racing back and forth in front of the bows of our leading craft. They got closer and closer until we had to either stop or collide with them. Then they opened fire and one of their boats rammed one of ours. They continued to ram our boats and one of our number started to list. Everyone kept well down as they continued to randomly fire their pistols at our boats. The situation worsened by the minute, as we were well outnumbered, and our defence boats were much smaller.

We saw a British destroyer suddenly come racing round the point. It was scary the way such a big ship moved. It was tilted right over as it turned, and had built up a huge wash on both sides of its big keel.

Ruben gave me the low down, as if I needed it. 'Shit! Here she comes. Type 45 Daring class destroyer, British Royal Navy. Speed up to 30 knots, about 60 km, and using all of it right now. Viper air defence system and top of the range radar makes her probably the most efficient fighting ship on the high seas today.'

'All right, Ruben, cool it,' barked his father. 'I hope they're friendly, but they're not saying much yet.'

'We're in a bad way, outnumbered and dwarfed by those launches. We are armoured. Even the Zodiacs are prepared to take gunfire, as they have armoured floats and multiple compartments. But if the destroyer, if its commander, has been compromised and takes their side, we're lost,' Ruben said in an unusually subdued tone.

Then Horatio shouted out. 'Prepare for evasive action! The fishing craft will sit, we'll run. It's us they're after anyway, the boy. We can run faster than they.'

Eustace was busy setting up his signalling equipment.

'Hold it, Major. The destroyer's signalling. They ask what are we carrying ?'

'Tell them a boy.'

Eustace signalled and read the reply,

'Strange bloody question, Major. Want to know his name.'

'Tell them Masuhun.'

The gunfire was getting heavier, and the occasional bullet slammed up against the Zodiac. We were all down behind the armour. Maria was trembling, not out of fear, though. I think she just trembled whenever she got nervous, so I held her tight.

Then all hell broke loose. The sirens on the destroyer started to wail, echoing loudly and eerily all across the bay, red lights flashing on and off throughout the ship. We could see her forward gun turrets move. She was huge and so frightening, a war machine, bristling with power and bearing down on us at a high speed.

'Action stations,' said Ruben. 'That's what those sirens are about. It's action stations. They're readying themselves and the ship for battle. Someone's really going to catch it now, and I hope it's not us.'

A loudspeaker's blaring staccato sound bounced across the waves.

'Unknown launches, this is the Destroyer Vengeful of her Majesty's Royal Navy. You are attacking craft flying under the flags of the kingdoms of Spain and Great Britain. Desist immediately, or we will open fire and blast you out of the water.'

And with the warning repeating over and over again, they opened fire.

'Warning shots,' cried Ruben. 'Over the bows of the launches. They're not playing games. And look, look!' he pointed with a hysterical shout.

Racing round the side of the destroyer, making a huge wake as they came, were two armoured Zodiac type landing craft filled with Royal marines ready for action as they tore at lightning speed towards the attacking launches, which turned tail and ran for the open sea. The water around us was churned up with the cross washes of the destroyer and the inflatables. We couldn't help it, everyone just stood or knelt up as best as they could and clapped and cheered.

Boadicea smiled and kissed Maria, then said, 'Well, Moon, or whatever your name is, someone up there really does love you.'

I smiled, not knowing how to answer. I was just a small unimportant boy from the North of Africa, and all these enormous things were happening around me—to me. I didn't know what to say. I just felt humble. But I needn't have worried with Ruben around.

'You can call him Moon, Moon is just fine, thanks, Bo,' he said with a grin.

'You keep out of it, Rube.'

The loudspeaker crackled back to life.

'Go find the Mother, Masuhun. Don't let them stop you now.'

'Thank you, Frank, again,' I shouted, knowing full well he would not hear me. I looked over and Eustace was signalling it.

'He says don't do anything stupid boy. Then he says bye.'

Gibraltar, Gateway to the World.

Small boats were still arriving in the bay as we continued across. Most carried banners, which Ruben, with his ever faithful field glasses, confirmed were emblazoned with emblems of a mother and child. It was scary. All of these boats were coming here to worship the mother and her baby, probably motivated to do so in a fashion similar to my own. It was getting more difficult to navigate the bay as a small flotilla. Approaching Europa, we found that dozens of boats were trying to embark on the Spanish side of the point. I could hear church bells, the sound floating mysteriously over the water as if it came from all around us. Rounding the point, we discovered that the situation was similar on the Trinity lighthouse landing and round the coast into the Mediterranean. Then Horatio came to a decision.

'Kids, as of now, disappear. Cover yourselves with blankets, lie down, and stay down, OK? Mahatma, contact shore and advise arrival of parcels at point three. Ask them to please be ready to convey to point one. Right now, we'll proceed all together to landing on the Spanish side of the point. At this juncture, the inflatables will peel off and head for Little Bay, leaving the large boats forcing an opening through the pilgrims' boats moored there. The idea is to get the three teams of five SB and SR guys landed. The three groups will force their way through the people. They're good people, it seems, but you never know who may be skulking amongst them. When people see your groups of five men, each wearing balaclavas and fatigues, and armed, they will give way.

You will scale the walls as planned, and carry your three dummies. Just cover them up so they look real. Once at the top, make your way to the shrine and set up a secure area for when we arrive.'

The bigger craft opened a way for us through the waiting mass of boats. I could see nothing from the bottom of our inflatable, but Eustace gave us a running commentary.

'United bloody nations, look at all those flags. French, Moroccan, Algerian, China, Vietnam. They're all there, dozens of nations represented. British, Dutch, Russian, mostly bloody foreigners. Probably all illegal immigrants, trying to get to Blighty. The British will stop them at the tunnel. Stiff upper lip, you know.' A muffled Ruben couldn't let it alone.

'What British? There's only Darwinders and Patels, the rest are all in Spain.'

'All right, Eustace, I think we've got the picture. Are the lads all ashore?'

'Yes, Major, and the first team has actually secured their stepladder and are climbing.'

So we left the three teams scaling the fortified fortress that was Europa Point, carrying their precious cargo, which was to all intents and purposes us. It was then that we heard the now familiar crackle of small arms fire start up.

'We continue as planned, the guys on shore are fifteen in number and backed up by our chaps arriving from Atunara, and soon from Rosia. Pilots, inflatables, set course for Little Bay. Let's go! Let's go! Other craft, make your way to Rosia Bay, where you can moor. People will be waiting for you. Over and out. And we, gentleman, again it's Little Bay. Arrival point three on your maps.'

The inflatables were now on their own, and moving at a steady but normal pace round the headland, direction Gibraltar harbour, destination Little Bay. Horatio wanted it to appear as if we were going to base after having dropped our cargo. In fact, the cargo, us, were lying hidden on the floor of one of the inflatables. The three teams of special forces men were carrying decoys to hopefully fool the enemy that we were on the backs of three very large men, scaling the bastion's walls.

They knew I was a kid, and we knew they would think of me as younger and smaller than I actually was. They weren't aware of who the other kids were, just that I was one of them. They wanted to kill me—a chilling thought—and would kill all three of us if necessary, just to make sure they got the right one. The continuous motion of the boat was making me feel nauseous. It really wasn't helped by the fact that we were lying under a pile of damp blankets and smelly tarpaulins. The boats slowed, and I could feel the keel grating onto what I imagined was a pebbly beach. As I felt it, I breathed a sigh of relief. The SB men who were still with us were off. I could feel and hear them as they plunged into the water, rushing the inflatables up the beach in what must have been an often practised operation.

'Come on, you lot, get lively. Nap's over.' Eustace was busying himself getting the blankets off us and getting us ashore.

It was a pebbly beach, flanked on two sides by rocky promontories, and enjoying a certain charm of its own. There must have been at least twenty bikes in all. Most of them had their engines running silently, the shimmer from the heat of their exhausts floating around them, and riders ready to roll. Black crash helmets were held out or sat waiting on the bike. The riders were all apparently expecting Horatio. As he stepped onto the beach, he smiled and gave a brief salute of sorts, a handshake to one of them, then a 'Hello, lads,' and off we went. We were each placed, with no explanation, on the back of a motorbike. There was a bike for Horatio, with Eustace as his passenger, and one for Boadicea with a man riding pillion. Mahatma rode in a car complete with earphones; he was still very much in control of everything that went down, even as it happened. The rest of our guys climbed speedily into the back of a waiting van. Out of the tiny lane leading to the bay, we turned right and up an incline to the dark opening of a tunnel hewn out of solid rock by Royal Engineers. It seemed fast, but I was unused to riding on a motorbike; this was the first time, in fact. We—that is, the three kids— were riding in the middle of the bunch, with Horatio, Boadicea, and a couple of other bikes leading the way. Suddenly, we were in the tunnel, the blackness lit up by strange coloured lights. I was very eager to get to wherever it was we were going, although I was worried. All this trouble, so many people, and so much organization. If nothing happened, I could just see Horatio and Boadicea pushing me off Europa Point with Ruben shouting, 'Don't come back, Moon.'

What were they expecting, anyway? I shut my eyes, and when I opened them, I was on a horse, holding onto an armour-clad figure riding in front of me. Around me were big armoured warhorses at full canter, carrying helmeted knights in white tunics, and clutching on for dear life were Ruben and Maria. Maria smiled at me and nodded as if to say, I also am seeing what you see.

And then we saw the end of the tunnel and daylight ahead, and as we emerged, the illusion disappeared; we were riding pillion again. In the far distance, but very clearly, I could see the Rif Mountains enshrouded in a light levanter mist and the North African coast. It took several minutes of negotiating a few lanes to arrive at the crowd blocking the access to the shrine. It was well past seven—nineteen hundred—and apparently Holy Mass had begun. They carried candles, whole families, children, old ladies, old men. Many of these people had come from a long distance away. They would have come in cars through the frontier, or walking, or over the sea in boats. What Eustace had said before was true, there were people from all races, Asiatics, blacks, Europeans, Arabs, and although I could not know it at that moment, I later discovered that they had indeed come from every country in the world. And there were many who looked like locals, devout people loving their virgin mother and her child, perhaps related to those who years ago had carried the Mother to safety. They, in their black veils and Sunday best, looked around bemused and apprehensive at the strange garb and alien features and appearance of the ever growing multitude that was invading their shrine and holy day. But many were smiling as if welcoming all and sundry with the famous Christian forbearance and affection for others that was bred into them. So we made our way as well as we could towards the shrine, the guys pushing their bikes and Maria and I walking together with Ruben.

'You saw them, too?' Maria asked.

I nodded. It began to drizzle very slightly, and we looked up for clouds, but there were none. I knew I was there, at the rock, the stone where the mother comes, and I knelt down. I felt fulfilled. I had managed to come to where my father had sent me. I saw a group of Muslims, I knew they were so by their dress, perhaps they had come over from their own mosque, the mosque of the two brothers, Ibrahim-Al-Ibrahim, across the way, right here at Europa Point. They knelt next to us, and I knew intuitively that they had come to join the Christians in revering their mother and child on the appointed day of the shrine. All around, people were kneeling and singing May songs of praise to the Mother. Without warning, the sky suddenly went dark, and it thundered loud and continuously for at least a minute, a long time for a peal of thunder. I could not see it, but surmised that it must have been a large dark cloud blocking the light of the sun. Although we should still be able to see with the astral twilight, it was pitch black. I thought it must be later than I had believed.

I heard an old lady cry out close to us. I put my head down and asked the mother and her son to look after my father. When I lifted my head, a light was shining from the sky, from nowhere, through the darkness and onto me, and people were shouting. Then the light grew and shone on us all and on the boats at sea and the Rif Mountains. It was an incredibly bright light. Then I saw the boats. There were so, so many. I could not see the seas for them, smaller and bigger, filling the bay and the ocean beyond for as far as my eyes could make out. There must have been millions of them.

I heard Maria's voice saying, 'It will be as the impact of a rogue asteroid upon an ocean. It has begun.'

Then all went silent, and I only heard the very gentle voice of a woman speaking to me, 'Go home, Masuhun. Your father lives.'

I put my head down and wept, and all around me I could hear people weeping and crying out.

I looked up—and saw her with her son.

I thought it must have been hours later when Maria hugged and kissed me.

'What happened, Maria? Was I sleeping?'
She took my head gently and looked into my eyes. Shaking her head from side to side, with the tears streaming from her eyes, she said, 'Go home, Masuhun. Your father lives.'

We fell against each other, weeping for joy because it was all real, and she had spoken to us.

And then, from amongst the crowds, a group of people, mainly young boys and girls of all nationalities, cultures, and races, came forward, some sheepishly pushed by their families who stood around them. They each looked at me and said in my ear, 'Masuhun?'

I said yes, and they would say, 'Go home, your father lives.'

And I, knowing they were my chosen brothers, kissed and embraced them and they would get emotional, as a great thing had occurred to us all. There were also older people, men and women, but the great multitude were young girls and boys. The hours must have passed by. Horatio, Mahatma, and the others just stood by, looking on not knowing, but knowing that they had witnessed something, something they would never see again.

And the chosen continued to come forward. Maria and I were taken away in military ambulances after four days and four nights, as we were exhausted and our ever-vigilant friends were fearing for our health. But the chosen continued to come. They continued, it seemed, for weeks. And to this day, nearly one year later, they still come.

Later, Horatio told me that the army commander had spoken to him to confirm that Europa Point had been militarily sealed off from the rest of Gibraltar, and that all residences and private property at the point were under military guard and protection. But the faithful would be allowed to come, and then return to their boats and depart. Apparently the official frontiers to the rock had also been sealed for two days because the influx of people was staggering.

Maria and I just sat there by the shrine for four days and four nights and embraced our brothers who came to tell Masuhun to go home, that his father lived. The people who lived around realized something monumental was occurring in their neighbourhood, and they brought us hot food, drinks, and blankets. But once Horatio felt we had had enough, he pulled us out. We were so exhausted that they carried us on stretchers to military ambulances. I called out for Ruben to be with us, as we felt incomplete without him.

He came to me and whispered in my ear, 'Go home, Masuhun. Your father lives. I saw her as well.' He added, with moist eyes, 'She wouldn't have dared leave me out.'

'We're going home, Moon. To your home. All of us, we're going to take you home.'

Then, just as I closed my eyes, I heard, 'Moon? Is there a stream or a small river close to where you live? Where we can lie in the cold water like we did that day and find peace? I'm so tired.'

Epilogue

Masuhun was taken to a waiting vessel named the MV Maria, skippered by a Gibraltarian ex-Royal Navy officer. It had been arranged for a local judge to meet them there. Masuhun was placed under arrest pending a hearing on extradition proceedings requested by the Spanish authorities regarding the murder of one Eduardo Garcia Canilla. He was, however, released on bail on his own recognizance and that of Major Horatio Bullock, retired, and Lieutenant Cmdr. Frank, also retired, currently captain and owner of the MV Maria. Following a flurry of diplomatic negotiations, the whole affair regarding eluding the Guardia Civil was filed away, although an investigation was initiated regarding the identity and patrons of the various mercenary bodies involved in the persecution of the boy Masuhun al-Rasheed.

Before legal proceedings took place, however, the extradition request was dropped by the Spanish authorities, as further evidence and witnesses had appeared to completely exonerate Masuhun.

The MV Maria arrived in the fishing port of .... on the North African coast, carrying on board a party headed by Major Horatio Bullock and Mrs. Boadicea, with a variety of family members and friends. They were transported in a small group of jeeps provided by the local Pasha, to whom letters of introduction had been presented, and who was delighted to cooperate. Masuhun's family were never advised

that he was coming, which resulted in an emotional and very tearful reunion. Masuhun's father, who had been in a profound coma since he had been attacked, had apparently, several days earlier, suddenly awoken from his coma, jumped out of his bed, and gone to the kitchen to make a cup of tea, Nana style. This was chronicled by his family, as it was so unexpected.
It happened at about twenty forty-five hours on the fifth of May.

The day after the reunion, Masuhun, together with his friends Maria, Ruben, Mahatma, Boadicea, and Horatio, went down to the beach to meet Ali and eat kefta. As usual, a group of black men were playing football. They apparently paused in their game when one of their number walked off the sand to where Masuhun was seated. It seems that the gentleman in question had tried to steal a ride on Masuhun's boat when he had first set out for Europe. They became inseparable friends and companions.

Masuhun, Ruben, and Maria all went back to school. Masuhun wanted to become a teacher in the Muslim and Christian traditions so that he would be as much at home in a madrassah school as a Catholic school. Ruben followed his father in a military discipline, whilst Maria wanted to be an agronomist so she could one day work with Mrs Rafiq in protecting the plant species of the world from evil.

But the impact made by the meteor had started its ripples, and they would not be stopped. Young philosophers, still in their teens some of them, could be seen in squares and rehabilitated public meeting places. Old adages started to return to replace those manipulative sayings imposed on the minds of children for the sake of expediency. For example: The end can never be said to always justify the means, as the means is part of the end, and the end a part of the means. Or that utopia is an achievable ideal.

As a direct result of whatever it was that actually happened on the fifth of May 2015 in Gibraltar and its surrounding seas, a series of events took place throughout the world that were termed by the press as the social upheavals of fifteen and sixteen.

Children from as young as the ages of five and upwards started to gradually reject the new technologies, and returned to play in streets and gardens with sticks, stones, tops, marbles, football coupons, imagination, and all those fascinating ideas that had once been the basis of their education as humans. Older members of society were progressively retired from their previously acquired status of social pariahs and potential paedophiles, and could be seen tottering around teaching children old games, jumping games, hiding games, and the whole kaleidoscope of games they had enjoyed as children, without the need for having to buy the latest technology to show them how to play. The resulting increase in attention given to these susceptible youths by the real and evil depraved criminals in our midst was swiftly combated by groups of youths who, in breach of the law, became vigilantes. A small happening such as the changed attitude of the children had an incredible effect on the whole of our society.

'The soul is healed by being with children.' (Fyodor Dostoyevsky)

Mothers and fathers began hurrying home earlier, at first to try to stop the kids from going out, and later, when they realised the kids were not going to stay in, to keep an eye on them, and then even later, to spend many an afternoon playing with the children or just sitting out in the cool evening chatting with other parents, something many of them had never done. Many mothers began to want to be real mothers again, and fathers to be real fathers.

The governments and big business were quick to react in many ways, at first negative in the extreme, such as telling the world that their children's education was suffering and that they would never become doctors and lawyers and architects. But the new mood eventually started to attract people of the traditional statesmen and women type. At a snail's pace, they eased into government, and it very slowly became apparent that a vibrant new road was being followed.

The first major enterprise was a United Nations ruling on birth control, so that the savage policies of overpopulation and forced sterilisation which had been in place, albeit secretly, would be replaced with logical ideas. Governments were economically castigated by the rest of humanity if they did not abide by the rules. The target was to stop the growth of the world's population in it's tracks, today, with fair allocation of permitted population for each country in the world.

Genetic sterilization of plant life or any living thing was strictly prohibited, with the direst penalties for companies, countries, or individuals who flew in the face of the prohibition.

Also to be eradicated, with all the force of the law and the power of united men and women throughout the world, was corruption in all its forms, and nepotism. Any state calling itself a democracy and yet placing a part of its population above the law, as was the case in Spain, would be taken to task and requested in the sternest of fashions to remove provisions such as these, which made a mockery of their so-called democracies. In Spain, around 100,000 people had not been subject to the normal courts of law, but only to the Tribunal Supremo. The members of the Supremo were voted in by the various political parties, who would negotiate amongst themselves to absolve transgressors.

'One of the saddest lessons of history is this: If we've been bamboozled long enough, we tend to reject any evidence of the bamboozle. We're no longer interested in finding out the truth.' (Carl Sagan)

Obviously, to mention Spain is but a case in point, there were many countries who needed to revise their laws.

Lobbying on behalf of big business, in all its shapes and forms, was declared strictly illegal, and the manipulation of foreign countries and their peoples at the whim of governments and major companies was to stop.

When the ripple was seen and its effects began to be felt, the world grew more confident in the possibility of stepping back from total destruction and the de-humanizing of its population. But it became more and more apparent that a huge swathe of humanity needed to change its ideas and philosophy. We needed to step back from aggression and relearn about humility, tolerance, compassion, and even love for our neighbours, and it was the kids who were beginning to push us in this direction.

'Few people are capable of expressing with equanimity, opinions which differ from the prejudices of their social environment. Most people are incapable of forming such opinions.' (Albert Einstein)

Another stick that was brandished at the new wave statespeople was economic. But it soon was demonstrated we had been lied to for a long time and that there were indeed other viable and sustainable economic models. These economic roads would not continue to enrich the very wealthy at the same rate as before, and their political implications would be a change, but they were workable.

Capitalism was accepted as a viable system by which to run a state. The only problem being all the cheating that went on, and of course the fact that the more money you had, the more capacity you had to find a way of breaking the rules. To counter this, an ethical committee made up of organisations such as Greenpeace and members of the general public was set up within the United Nations to act as watchdogs for cheating. The penalties were very severe for those involved.

Right and left sensibly concurred that the excessive spending and sharing of wealth in many cases to those who preferred to live off the state was no answer to anything, as was employing half of the country's population in civil service. People were thereafter educated from a young age to be a positive contributing member of the society they lived in.

One of the main changes embarked upon was a gradual stepping up of the search for natural and sustainable energy resources. The investment and technological might of the planet was put towards the fight to create an everlasting source of clean energy, with various possibilities in play, including nuclear fusion, which was hardly a new concept. And of course the agenda of the multi-nationals and oil and gas producing countries was now relegated to second place. The priority was the well-being of humanity as a whole.

A special law was passed, and adopted by legislatures throughout the world, protecting the wave of young philosophers. Their influence on the main body of humanity was extremely gradual, as the mainstream was very reluctant to change. That mainstream had been the consumer dictators' greatest ally, and the new doctrines being propounded by the youngsters would lead to the disintegration of this social form and its replacement by individualism. This ideal was potentially the scourge of all organised religions, or rather their enhancement, as religions were not attacked. Instead, it was suggested that they were, all of them, corridors to the Lord.

'In individuals, insanity is rare; but in groups, parties, nations, and epochs, it is the rule.' (Frederick Nietzsche)

'It is no measure of health to be adjusted to a profoundly sick society.' (Jiddu Krishnamurti)

'Imagine a society that subjects people to conditions that make them terribly unhappy, then gives them the drugs to take away their unhappiness. Science fiction is already happening in our society.' (Theodore J. Kaczynski)

www.ingramcontent.com/pod-product-compliance
Lightning Source LLC
Chambersburg PA
CBHW060336310726
48976CB00007B/2584